EARL OF BERGEN

MAKE MINE AN EARL SERIES
BOOK 2

ANNA ST CLAIRE
USA TODAY BESTSELLING AUTHOR
with LAUREN HARRISON

EARL OF BERGEN
PUBLISHED BY: SASSY ROMANCES

Copyright © 2019 by Anna St. Claire
All rights reserved.

Cover Design by Joanna D'Angelo
Edited by Heather King

For my grandma, Anna,
who gave me my love of reading and writing,
and whose love I will never forget.

~and~

For those willing to see the 'possibilities' and take a chance on love and
happiness ever after
and to those that support them.

ACKNOWLEDGMENTS

Thank you to my own special 'hero,' Roger.
There's a part of Roger in all my heroes.
He reads every one of my stories
and always gives me valuable feedback.

CHAPTER 1

STONY STRATFORD, ENGLAND ~ 1817

*D*euced tired of traveling in the freezing wet weather, Lord Thomas Bergen urged his horse onto High Street in the direction of one of the baiting houses. The journey home had been especially tedious this time, thanks to the nasty weather. He should have expected it, so close to Christmas. It was lucky that it had not started snowing. The skies seemed to threaten that very misfortune.

His horse stopped, prompting him to make a choice. "You know me too well, my girl." He sniggered and patted her neck. The two inns he patronized stood almost next door to each other—both offered pleasurable entertainment and a hearty meal; he had enjoyed many a good time at both.

Noise accompanied a couple of over-served men as they were tossed through the door of the Bull Inn into the road in front of him, thus making his decision for him.

"Ah...the Bull Inn seems to be lively tonight. 'Tis exceedingly tempting, but somewhat more than I am ready to take on tonight." He laughed out loud as if conversing with his mare. "It will be the Cock

Inn for me this night, Merry." With that, he patted his horse and nudged her towards a post outside the inn. At his approach, a young ostler straightened from a position against the wall and he handed the reins over. Fishing in his waistcoat pocket, Bergen withdrew a shilling for the groom. "Take good care of Merry, and I will match this in the morning. What is your name, lad?"

"Perry, my lord," the young man answered, taking the proffered reins. "I'll do an especially fine job with her—I'll rub her down, and feed her, and I'll make sure she gets a warm blanket."

Bergen chuckled. "I'm sure you will. Is there anyone here who could check her shoes? We stumbled over a rut in the road a few miles ago, and I noticed her gait was uneven for a while afterward. She may need a hind one replaced or tightened."

"Certainly, my lord. Smitty is still here and will be happy to look her over for you."

"Thank you, lad. Merry will give you no trouble." He patted his dappled grey mare and grabbed his saddlebag. He had thought the journey would take only a day, but the weather had considerably mired the road. A good night's sleep for both of them would be just the ticket.

Loud music, raucous singing, and the smell of mutton assailed him upon entering the inn. His stomach reacted quickly, growling loudly. *Yes, I will feel better shortly*, he thought to himself. *A hearty meal and a good night's sleep would feel wonderful.*

The innkeeper and his wife—a short round man and an almost matching woman—greeted him. "Good evening, my lord. How can we serve ye?"

"I need a room and a good meal." Bergen smiled in anticipation.

"Do ye think ye be staying more than a night?"

"Just tonight, thank you." Bergen looked towards the tap-room and surveyed the merriment. It would be the wee hours of the morning before that settled down. "Do you have a room available that is not over the main room down here?"

"Certainly, we do, my lord. Would ye like your meal and a hot bath brought up for ye, my lord?" the missus asked. Without giving him a moment to respond, she continued, "We be serving lamb stew and I made fruit cake special for tonight. 'Tis the Christmas season, after all, and we are starting to do some of our cooking. Lamb be my husband's favourite dish, isn't that right, William?" She gently nudged him with her elbow.

The innkeeper started. "Yes, yes, dearest wife." He coughed and stood straighter. "Lord Bergen, it is good to see ye. It has been too long."

"Thank you. It is good to see you and your wife looking so well." He smiled at the wife. "And lamb is also my favourite dish, so 'tis a lucky thing for me that I stopped here this night." The innkeeper's wife smiled broadly at his remarks.

"Did Lord Weston come with ye?" The innkeeper walked to the door and glanced out.

"No, Lord Weston is not with me on this occasion." Bergen was not sure where this was going but appreciated that the man seemed to like both Edward and him. Maybe the room would be decent. The last time they had stayed here there had been live female entertainment… all night. A smile tugged at his mouth at the memory. The girl had been a pretty one—he could not recall her name, but he could easily recollect the low cut of her gown.

"Yes, well, Lord Weston is probably just returning from his honeymoon." He glanced down at his muddy boots and frowned. "I am making a bit of a mess in the entrance, here. A bath would be most welcome, thank you. I will then take my meal in the private dining room, providing there is a table available."

"Oh, yes, my lord. There is a table available in our private parlour. Ye will not have to suffer the insolence of those in the tap-room. My missus will show ye to your room."

A tub of hot water was just what he needed, he thought, as he undressed in the quiet room overlooking the coach house. It was a simple room—single bed, a wooden stand with a sink, and a chair. A large single-sash curtained window was on the wall next to the bed. The dark shabby grey curtains did not add much ambiance to the room. There was a full moon out tonight and the light of the moon would be preferable to the darkness of the room, he thought. He wished he had thought to open them before settling into the tub. The innkeeper's wife had thoughtfully sent him sandalwood soap with clean towels. He eased further down into the water and closed his eyes, happy to empty his mind of all thoughts. Before many minutes had passed, however, loud female and male laughter, accompanied by raucous singing, drifted in through the window, which he suddenly realized was cracked open behind that set of shabby grey curtains. He sunk further into the warm tub and found himself following a strange conversation. He could smell the smoke from a campfire and imagined that there must be one in a clearing in the wood behind the inn. *I will look when I finish my bath.* The voices were carrying clearly on the night air, despite the distance.

"I swear, 'tis that cursed donkey. Ever since we picked him up, bad things have happened. He goes no further," a deep male voice bellowed above the laughter.

"You're just blaming your shortcomings on the donkey. He isn't to blame for your inadequacy," a female responded with a loud cackle.

"Woman, I'm done with you. Leave me. Go mind the children. You know what I am talking about. I have not been able to sell a single horse, and I am not the only one who is noticing the bad luck. That donkey is cursed and he's spreading it among us."

"The donkey is a baby."

"Oh, for God's sake! We got him and we lost the horses we were going to trade. His braying and...singing scared them off." A loud mimic of a donkey braying to 'Rock-a-bye baby' followed. Loud laughter erupted.

"I 'ave never seen a singing donkey before," a loud husky voice added with a hoot. "The women love him."

"The amulet around his neck is evil. I tell you, the donkey is cursed," the deep male voice thundered.

"Well, the horses did disappear, but that was because the gate was left open. Donkey had nothing to do with..."

"What are you talking about? We never leave the gates open.

Never. I do not care…that thing around his neck…has magic. He is cursed. We leave him. That is the end of this discussion."

Bergen could hear female voices speaking in a soothing and sing-song fashion yet could not make out anything else beyond their laughter. His bath water had grown cold, so he rinsed his face and stood up. The stream of cold night air that had offered him so much entertainment moments ago now created almost quaking shivers. Quickly, Bergen dried himself on a towel and dressed. He needed his dinner. *A singing donkey? A* cursed *singing donkey? What do these people drink?* He needed some of that, he mused, as the foolish questions formed in his head, and then…a good night's sleep. He went to shut the window when a soft singing captured his attention. Instead, he pulled a frayed cane chair from beside the door to the window and doused his light, and instantly found himself drawn to the fire-lit images of eight women dancing provocatively around a campfire. *Damn it! I wish I had ordered my meal up here, after all.*

The moon gave just enough light to make out the details of their lithe bodies. The gypsies were obviously enjoying themselves. No one seemed to care that they were camping so close to a building, which gave him more time to observe. With a laugh, he slouched to a comfortable sitting position. *By George, I never thought I would be a Peeping Tom, but I cannot ignore the allure of their exotic…dance.* In spite of the distraction, though, before long he was losing the battle with his eyelids.

A bright, rising sun woke him, and he found himself slumped in the chair. The room was freezing cold, owed to the window still open. Laughing to himself at his predicament, he tried to stand, pushing through the aches and pains of an acquired stiff back, so he stood and stretched. *When was the last time I slept in a chair?* He surveyed his clothing and decided to do his best to freshen before breakfast. As quickly as he could, he poured water in a bowl and cleaned up. He laughed out loud thinking of what his valet would say if he could see him trying to tie a fashionable knot with his cravat, until he gave up and made some sort of tied bow. His stomach was rumbling loudly as he hurried down to the dining room to break his fast.

An hour later, Perry was brushing Merry when Bergen arrived at the stables ready to leave. Merry looked rested enough.

"Thank you, lad." Bergen nodded and when his mare was saddled, passed the ostler two more shillings before riding away in the direction of London. He needed to be there by tomorrow for he had promised Aunt Faith he would be there. Otherwise, he would have stayed here an extra day. Stony Stratford always held a good time. Besides, the Season would be long and dreary without his friends. They had all fallen into parson's mousetrap. He still could not believe Edward was married. It had been an inn like this where they had first seen the young woman who would become his friend's wife—Miss Hattie. Her cursing parrot had certainly been refreshing. Yet once the popinjay had set his sights on Edward, there had been nothing else for it. The very thought filled Bergen with mirth. Bound and determined, the bird had been, to have them both.

A loud braying caught his attention as he rounded the bend out of town. Merry jerked in distaste.

"Steady, girl. What have we here?" A small grey donkey was braying loudly and kicking up his heels, unable to free himself from ropes tying him to a large mulberry bush. His thrashing had torn off limbs, but not the core of the bush, where the ropes were secured.

Bergen slid from his horse. "Just a minute, little fellow." He tried to sort out the muddle of rope and branch that the donkey had created. "You must be the little donkey I heard about last night. I recall they said you were cursed."

"Eeeeeeeorrrrrrr!" Kicked-up clumps of mud covered them both.

"Damn it, donkey! I am trying to help. Hold still."

The donkey tried to turn his head towards him and seemed to be moving his lips as if pleading. Bergen did not sense any aggression.

"There, now. That should do it." Still holding the rope, he freed the donkey and patted him on the rump, hoping to send him on his way, but the donkey stayed. He pulled up his lips and showed his teeth.

"Oh, there! Is that a smile? I have never seen a smiling donkey... and with blue eyes..." Bergen laughed out loud. "Well, your eyes do not quite line up, but you are a friendly fellow despite your predicament. Not the temper I have normally experienced with your brethren, I will say."

Bergen fished in his saddlebag and pulled out an apple he had packed before leaving on the trip. "Here you go...Clarence. You look like a Clarence, I think."

The donkey accepted the apple and nudged Bergen's arm in a gentle show of thanks.

"Very well...off with you, Clarence. Time for me to go." The donkey starred at Bergen and slowly walked off in the opposite direction.

Once back in his saddle, Bergen urged Merry into a canter. "I am suddenly in a good mood, old girl. I have done a good deed today." He began to whistle and suddenly heard what sounded like a donkey braying along to his song. Bergen turned slowly. There stood Clarence, smiling his odd smile.

"Clarence, what *am* I to do with you?" He looked upward at the position of the sun. It had to be two hours past his early meal already and he had hoped by this time to be well underway. He could not take a donkey into London with him, so there was nothing to do but retrace his steps to the inn. Grabbing up the rope, he looped it through Clarence's collar. "That is an interesting collar you have, Clarence. Does it mean anything significant?" The words of the gypsy came back to him. *Amulet, cursed.* "Well, it is odd, but I do not think I have ever heard of a cursed donkey. I think you might be the funniest one I have met, however."

A thunderous sound exited the small animal; soon they were both enveloped with a sulphuric stench.

"Goodness, Clarence! Was that you...good God!" Bergen grappled with the ropes while at the same time trying to move away from the animal.

"Whew! All right now, let us go back."

On reaching the Cock Inn, Bergen noticed Perry in the yard and whistled. A deep bray mimicked him from behind. Unable to stop himself, he laughed.

"Yes, my lord? Are you returning for the night?"

"No…I found myself in the company of this…Clarence."

"A donkey?" The young man smiled in amusement. "You named him Clarence?"

"Yes. It seemed to fit." Bergen chuckled. "Clarence seems in need of a home."

"Oh, I see, my lord. Well, the master here already has a donkey for his cart and though I shouldna say so, he is a bit of a skinflint. I do not think he would take to this little fellow, but there is a place…" Perry scratched his head and smiled.

"Lady Newton in the big house up the lane, there…" He pointed towards the other end of the High Street. "…she takes in strays. She heals them and gives them a home. Been known to take all kinds of animals. I reckon she'd like this little donkey—er, Clarence."

"Thank you, Perry. Could you give me a better description of her house?"

"My lord, it be the first one you see as you pass out of town. On the right, it is. It has a short, black iron fence surrounding it, and the yard is full of plantings—I think roses. Yes, red ones." He nodded, seeming pleased with his directions.

"Thank you, again, Perry. You are very helpful." Bergen turned to Clarence.

"Well. old boy, it appears we are going to make a social call. This should be interesting." He gently tugged at the donkey, but before he would move, Clarence turned to smile at Perry.

"Lizzie!" Aunt Jane shouted from the back door, loud enough for anyone in the county to hear. "There is a delicious gentleman arrived!"

Elizabeth cast her gaze heavenward. Aunt Jane thought any human with different parts and of marriageable age was delicious. Dear Horace had only been dead for two years, and Jane never tired of trying to see Elizabeth remarried.

"I will be there directly," Elizabeth replied as she shut the door with her foot and set down the pail of fresh milk without spilling it. The milkmaid was away, caring for her ailing mother, so Elizabeth had taken on the extra task. She did not mind, really. There was something soothing about the repetitive tasks of farm work.

After untying her apron, she placed it back on the hook beside the door and made a fool's attempt to tidy her hair.

"Why bother," she muttered, "Most likely it is only Jed Hamm come to convince me to give the children away."

They had gone 'around and around' her propensity to take in helpless children and animals, and he was constantly haranguing her about giving them to an orphanage in London. Building her ire as she walked up to the drawing room from the kitchen, she was ready to go to war with him by the time she was at the door to the formal room where they received their guests. It was bright with white, blue and light touches of yellows with fresh daisies in vases around the room.

"Jed Hamm, if you are here to argue again, I will not have it!" she said, bursting through the door, stopping short. "I beg your pardon. You are not Squire Hamm."

Aunt Jane snorted in a most unladylike fashion. She was an octogenarian who found it convenient to pretend she had a few screws loose in order to say what she liked. She was a dear.

"I have not had the pleasure, no," a deep, seductive voice said from above. She craned her neck to look upwards at least a foot, into a handsome face with blue eyes and blond hair. *Delicious indeed.*

"My name is Bergen, my lady; at your service." He made an elegant leg, as Aunt Jane would say, and Elizabeth did her best not to stare at his finely shaped calves and thighs, which were in complete contrast to the spindly limbs borne by the Squire. She shook her head.

"I am Elizabeth Newton. How may I be of service?" As beautiful as this man was, she had no time for silly dreams. By the look of him, the man was a London dandy and was, in all likelihood, very aware of his charms.

"I happened upon a stray animal, and I was told you were just the person to see."

She could feel her brow knit together. Who had been speaking to the stranger about her?

"If I have offended you, I beg your pardon." He reached up and made to wipe away a speck of dirt before pulling his hand back.

Elizabeth flushed at his forwardness. She did recall from her days in London that the men were flirtatious. What a country bumpkin he must think her, but there was something seductive in his touch which made her feel heat in places that Horace never had.

"Was I misinformed?

Elizabeth cleared her throat. "No, I do have a tendency to acquire helpless creatures."

"Excellent. Then may I show you what I have found?"

"Of course." Elizabeth indicated for him to lead the way while she glanced at Aunt Jane, who was beaming and making hand signals behind his back. Elizabeth cast a warning look for her aunt to behave before turning back to Mr. Bergen. Or was it, Lord Bergen? *He must be a lord!* She would have to mind him closely. He would not be the first to think her widowed status meant she was free with her favours.

He waited for her to pass through the door through the kitchens, stopping by the larder to retrieve an apple, before following her down the steps into the sunshine.

"Over here," he said as he held out his hand towards a beech tree to the side of the drive.

"A donkey? You found a stray donkey?" she asked in disbelief as she surveyed the dwarfed and odd-looking specimen. A small grey donkey stood in front of her. He had larger ears than she had seen on donkeys and blue eyes. One eye appeared crossed.

"Well, not precisely. He was abandoned by some gypsies at the inn where I was staying. I overheard them speak of leaving him."

She folded her arms and looked at him sceptically. "The circus troupe? They are more wont to take than to leave anything behind."

"They think he is cursed..." Bergen held out his hands. "...which is nonsense, of course."

"How delightful," she said dryly, even though she could use a donkey. They were known to be excellent protectors of herds, and a fox had killed a lamb recently.

"Does he have a name?"

Lord Bergen hesitated. "Clarence."

Elizabeth narrowed her eyes. "Did you say, 'Clarence'?"

He held up his hands in defence. "He looks like a Clarence."

Elizabeth stepped closer and the donkey bared his teeth at her. She jumped back. "Oh!"

"He will not hurt you," Bergen reassured her, stepping forward and scratching behind the donkey's ears. "I think he might be smiling at you."

Elizabeth looked at him uncertainly, but stepped forward again and since the donkey was distracted with Lord Bergen, she patted the mealy coloured nose. Clarence showed his teeth again.

"I do think you are correct. He does appear to be smiling. How peculiar!"

"Everything about him is peculiar. No offence intended, Clarence," he said to the animal. "But he does seem to be good-natured."

"A characteristic ne'er visited upon any other donkey I have ever met," Elizabeth retorted. "He is quite small, but that should not matter if I do not harness him to a cart. Where did you say you found him?"

"Tied to a mulberry bush near the inn I was staying at."

"You poor dear," Elizabeth said as she took a piece of apple she had in her pocket and fed it to him.

"He is yours now, whether you want him or not," Bergen said with a laugh. "I fed him an apple and he has followed me since."

"That will surprise no one. I am in the habit of adopting strays."

"Why do you, if you do not mind me asking?"

She waved a hand. "I can, so I do. The poor creatures cannot help their sad circumstances."

"How many *poor creatures* do you have, precisely?"

She wrinkled her brow and tapped her cheek with an index finger. "Let me see... Sheep, cows, horses, chickens, goats, pigs, five—no, six —dogs and ten cats, I think." She threw up her hands. "I have no idea!"

"It sounds no more unusual than any farm," he said, unconvinced.

"Yes, but they are not all, well...*well*...and then there are the children."

"May I enquire how many children you have?" he asked politely.

"Only three of those, but they..." Clarence made the most horrific gaseous sound, interrupting her answer. Although she could not keep her eyes from widening in dismay, it was too funny to contain her laughter.

CHAPTER 2

"*L*izzie! It is so very cold outside. Do invite this young gentleman in and let him get warm. After all, he did bring you a gift." The older woman did not wait for agreement. "Come in, sir." She stepped back and waved Bergen into the entrance hall. Turning to Lady Newton, she whispered, none-too-quietly, "Yes, indeed, Elizabeth...he is a very fine young gentleman." She slowly emphasized her words.

Bergen had to bite his tongue to keep from laughing aloud at the woman's candid appraisal. Lady Newton's face turned a beautiful shade of pink at the woman's comment and she turned away for a moment. He glanced at the thin wiry woman that stood beside her. Her once long dark hair was now white and pulled tight away from her face in some sort of bun that he could not see. Her well-lined face spoke years of laughter and life, and her faded blue eyes sparkled with mischief. Based on the smile that seemed to emanate behind her eyes, he sensed she delighted in poking society in the nose with her candour.

"Yes, my lord." Turning again to face him, Lady Newton gave a welcoming smile. "Please come in. May I offer you some tea? Aunt Jane is quite right, the wind is truly frigid when one stands still. We can finish our discussion inside. Please, join us and warm yourself." She stepped back, allowing him to enter.

Well, this is getting more pleasing by the moment, Bergen thought. It *was* cold, but he was finding himself more and more enchanted by the petite buxom blonde as each minute passed. Getting to know Lady Newton suddenly seemed more important than even warming himself by the fireplace.

Lady Newton's blue-green eyes held his for a moment—probably longer than was acceptable, but he could not help it. Despite her aunt's uproarious verbal exchanges, she had managed to maintain absolute composure. He could not remember when he had found himself so attracted to a woman in so short a time.

Aunt Jane was very diverting, and Lady Newton's seriousness seemed the perfect contrast for her eccentric aunt—their exchanges alone were worth the trip here. He thought of his own Aunt Faith and chuckled to himself—the two aunts could have been sisters, if he had not known better. Both were peevish octogenarians, and recalling his own aunt's words, not trusting of 'modern namby-pamby ways.' Thinking of his own relative recalled to his mind the reason for his journey. Bergen needed to get back on the road to London. Aunt Faith would be looking for him…but maybe there was no immediate cause for haste.

Bergen accepted the offer. "Tea would be most welcome. It is rather chilly out here." Upon entering the narrow hall, he paused by an old walnut table and removed his greatcoat, gloves and hat—the coat and hat Lady Newton hung upon a hook on the wall. The gloves she laid on the table. Curious, he looked around; *there seemed to be no servants…*

The two ladies led him to a blue and white parlour, just off the entrance hall. A dark pianoforte sat in front of a brightly lit picture window, framed by white lace curtains. Aunt Jane took a seat on a comfortable-looking light blue velvet couch which was nestled against the back wall. It perfectly matched the light blue and white toile wall covering. A silver tea service with blue and white patterned teacups sat ready on a side-table. He noticed the daisies and figured them a favourite flower of Lady Newton.

"Thank you for the invitation…Aunt Jane. May I call you Aunt Jane?"

"Certainly, my dear." Turning to her niece, she whispered loudly, "Lizzie, do try to be conciliating. This is as much for me as for you." She continued, "We do not get many delightful-looking gentlemen visiting these days, you know. My niece may be too prudish to show any interest, but I should like to feast these old eyes for a while!" She patted the cushion nearest to her. "Here…sit beside me, young man. I cannot abide these modern milk-and-water manners."

"*Aunt Jane!*" Lady Newton hastily took the seat next to her aunt. "Lord Bergen, I think you might be comfortable in this chair." She pointed to a high-backed chair adjacent to the couch.

"Ah, thank you." Bergen cleared his throat. He wanted to become acquainted with her, but she was being tormented by the aunt. Still, he ventured to ask, "Will Clarence be the first donkey to join the other inhabitants of the farm, do you think?"

"I do believe so." Lady Newton smiled. "I have noticed he is a very personable little fellow—one with uncanny timing too." At that remark, they both laughed.

He appreciated the way her dimples framed the corners of her mouth when she smiled.

This is a pleasant distraction; certainly better than the lonesome ride to London I had planned to make today.

"I believe you said the animals you keep are not all well? How do you care for them?" he asked.

"I have some help with the animals. The children do quite a bit, but mostly I care for them myself. I enjoy it." Her voice had suddenly become animated. Obviously, this was something the lady truly revelled in doing.

"I would be very interested in seeing how Clarence takes to them all. I can imagine a singing donkey could be very useful, no offence to our absent Clarence," he lightly teased, suddenly glad to have met the donkey. *How else would I have found myself in such delightful company? Aunt Faith will have to wait. Surely, she can spare me a day here.*

"My lord, we take *all* animals—big, small, with one ear or both," quipped Aunt Jane, suddenly fanning her face with what seemed an exaggerated look of exasperation. "My niece has a big heart and cannot turn down an animal that seems lost or down on its luck."

Lady Newton shot her aunt a critical look. "What Aunt Jane means, sir, is that we have taken in many injured animals, and a couple of them were missing an ear or a maybe a leg. Nevertheless, those we could heal, have adapted. They live here. I love helping the animals...and once here, they stay. This is their home."

"Humph! By best accounts, we have a menagerie out here—the only creature we do not have is a man." Aunt Jane slapped her knee and began to laugh at her own quip, while her niece blushed a deep shade of red.

"Aunt Jane! Really!" Lady Newton paused and took a deep breath. "I think every animal deserves a chance." She turned and whispered loudly to her aunt. "Please behave."

Wearing a mischievous smile, Aunt Jane seemed unscathed by the light admonishment and persisted. "You deserve a chance, too, my Lizzie."

"Aunt Jane...*please.* Lord Bergen does not wish to hear such... nonsense." She turned to Bergen while holding the sugar tongs. "Do you care to allow me to sweeten it for you, my lord?"

He grinned. This was the best morning he had had in a while. Who knew a donkey could be responsible for such joy? "Yes, please." His journey to London would unquestionably wait a day more.

Bergen nodded at the pianoforte by the window. "Do you play, Lady Newton?"

"She is excellent at the pianoforte...and has a lovely voice," her aunt remarked, clearly proud of her niece's talent.

Lizzie—Lady Newton—seemed a little too silent to him.

Feeling a palpable tension in the air, Bergen decided, with regret, it was time to go. He could only imagine the conversation these two would have once he had left.

He realized he had not bothered to ask Perry what Smitty had found with Merry's shoes before he himself had left the inn this morning. How lame he had been! Probably it was due to his lack of sleep from the nocturnal spying he had done by his window. He had gone to bed without food, for goodness' sake. And this morning, he had been so anxious to get underway to London after sating his hunger, he had completely forgotten to inquire. He would return to the inn and ask, as well as secure a room for another night.

"Ladies, I am afraid I must quit this delightful visit and return to town. I have a few matters to take care of before riding on to London."

He had hoped for more occasion to foster an acquaintance with this enticing young woman and decided to further his cause another way. Maybe an opportunity to spend time with her would show itself.

"Lady Newton—" He paused and took a breath before continuing, "If you are amenable, I should like to contribute towards Clarence's keep." He hoped he was giving her proper address. There was no way to know with the little information he had gleaned. Although he seemed to remember—now he came to think of it—Perry had so designated her, it could have been mere courtesy. She could be a lady. Yet he did not recognize the name, Newton, as that of a peer.

"Nonsense, I would not dream of it, sir." Elizabeth set down her spoon. "'The animals give me so much pleasure—they always give more to us than we do to them."

And she was not giving him any more information.

"Dinner!" Aunt Jane proclaimed suddenly. "You must join us for dinner tonight, sir. I insist upon it." Bergen bit his lip to hold back a grin. They were certainly an entertaining pair, and his appreciation for Aunt Jane was growing. He would like nothing better than to spend time with this blonde beauty and become better acquainted. Having already realized he wanted more time with Lady Newton, Bergen gave the pretence of deliberation before answering. Turning to her, he responded, "I should love to join you, ma'am, but may I ask if you would be so kind as to provide us with a song or two after dinner?"

"Well, I... Very well, if you wish. I do hope you will not be disappointed. Aunt Jane is somewhat prone to exaggeration." Another sweet, pink blush coloured her face.

I have an invitation to dinner! He wanted to sing, himself, so pleased he was!

"Dinner is at six." Lady Newton nodded, suddenly seeming shy.

"Then I will be on my way, ladies." Bergen bowed to Aunt Jane as her niece rose to her feet. "I appreciate your hospitality and your willingness to give Clarence a home, Lady Newton. He will be very happy here."

"He will be a welcome addition, I assure you."

Together they retraced their steps to the entrance hall, where a tall aging butler he had not seen previously handed him his greatcoat and hat and opened the door for him.

"I will look forward to dinner with you and your family this evening."

"I do hope we are not delaying you from important business. I fear a quiet country dinner is not what you are accustomed to."

Lady Newton seemed to relax at his leaving. Perhaps it was because she would be getting a slight break from her aunt's antics. He grinned at the thought. "I am sure it will be everything which is delightful, ma'am."

"Goodbye, Lord Bergen. I will go at once to introduce Clarence to his new friends."

Bowing once more, he regained the road, gathering the reins from the garden fence he had gently looped it around and mounted his horse. A long, woeful bray made him turn around in time to see Clarence running from the side of the house towards him.

"Whoa there, Merry, my girl," he said, stroking her brown neck. It seemed that Merry was not one of Clarence's supporters. "Clarence, your home is here, now." He slid from his horse again and patted the errant donkey.

"Eeeeoorre." The frantic donkey shook his head wildly back and forth and tried to grab Bergen's greatcoat with his teeth. "Eeeeoorre."

"Is he refusing? Is that no…from a donkey?" Bergen asked, filled with mirth.

"Oh, dear." Lady Newton quickly followed and gently tugged on the loose piece of rope still hanging from the donkey's collar. "Clarence...Lord Bergen plans to return this evening to give a proper goodbye. We want you to stay. You will have many friends here."

Bergen studied her manner as she spoke to the animal and marvelled that the donkey immediately became still. Could Clarence understand what was being said? *That is just fustian nonsense. A donkey does not understand words.* Lady Newton pulled Clarence close to her leg and softly rubbed his head, soothing him.

"You have a way with animals, Lady Newton. I am astonished at the way you are able to communicate with him." He nodded a silent thank you. "I shall see you fine ladies this evening. You too, Clarence," he added soothingly.

Leaving through the ornate iron entrance gate, he turned Merry towards town with a whistle on his lips. He was sure Perry could give him some information. The boy seemed to know a great deal about a lot of things beyond his sphere.

As Bergen neared the turn in the road where he had found Clarence, he saw something large dart into the bushes. From the shape, it looked like a man, but he could not be sure. He slowed Merry down and felt for his small silver pistol in his coat pocket. Surely, he would not have to deal with a highwayman after such a glorious morning. As he passed the mulberry bush, he heard voices yet saw no further movement. A male and female were arguing, but he could not make out the words. The tones did seem familiar...not unlike the voices he had heard the night before outside his window. Not looking for trouble, he nudged Merry on. There was no sign of the gypsy tribe. *How curious that they were where I found Clarence,* he mused. Instinct warned him that something was not right. He would also have to ask Perry about the gypsy troupe.

ELIZABETH HAD no need for a London dandy, and she was trying not to be resentful of Aunt Jane for inviting him to dinner. He was too handsome by half and she had never been wont to partake in frivolous flirtations. Nevertheless, she refused to be uncivil and it was only for one dinner. That did not mean she could not convince him she was not to his taste, though. She had seen his eyes roaming over her in curiosity and he already thought her eccentric, so why not prove him correct?

"Which dress will you wear, my lady?" her abigail asked, holding up two gowns for her perusal.

"The grey poplin with the high neck."

"You have not worn that since you put off your blacks!" her old nursemaid said in disbelief.

Elizabeth raised a haughty eyebrow. She did not wish to be questioned when she was already feeling insecure. She was not normally so prim.

"As you please, my lady."

"And please have Sally bring the children. They will be joining us for dinner."

"With a guest?" Hannah asked with the familiarity of an old retainer.

"He will not mind. He likes animals and children. Besides, he will not be here long. The vicar is also coming to discuss the Christmas pageant, so the children should be there."

"As you wish, my lady." Hannah tightened the laces on Elizabeth's gown and left the room. Elizabeth should probably be ashamed, but she had seen enough of these London bucks to know the type, and he might as well know what things were really like here so he could be on his way.

When she went downstairs, she was surprised to find Bergen and Aunt Jane on the sofa, having a tête-à-tête. Her white cat, Snowflake, was sitting in Lord Bergen's lap purring and swishing his tail. Elizabeth had never seen the cat come near anyone but Aunt Jane. Meanwhile, the bull mastiff, Sampson, was curled up at his feet. Aunt Jane was regaling Bergen with stories of her youth, and he was smiling at her as if she were in the bloom of her first Season.

"I see you have met some of our menagerie," Elizabeth said as she entered the room determined not to be taken in by his charm.

He made to stand but she waved him back down. "The rest of the party will join us shortly. The vicar is coming to discuss the Christmas pageant and the children will be joining us."

Aunt Jane let out an inhuman growl before turning it into a half-hearted cough.

"You must not think so ill of him," Elizabeth gently reprimanded.

"He is a fat, old toad who does not preach real sermons," she returned peevishly.

"Aunt, it is long past time to let bygones be bygones. He has replanted the garden he accidentally killed, as well as a portion of the adjoining hedge."

Aunt Jane gave a disdainful sniff.

"I think his sermons are very thoughtful and lovely. No one wants to hear hell-fire and brimstone all the time, anyway," Elizabeth added.

Aunt Jane shrugged a shoulder begrudgingly. Elizabeth noticed Lord Bergen looked very amused.

"May I pour you a drink, sir?" she asked.

"No, thank you. I am quite content. I am curious as to where all the misfit animals are, however. All of these seem perfectly normal."

"They are here and there. I am certain some more will make an appearance."

The vicar, who really did look like a pudgy little toad, arrived then and Elizabeth made the introductions before the children were brought into the drawing room by their nurse.

"Children, come make your bows to our new guest, Lord Bergen, and you know Vicar Brown, of course."

"Lord Bergen, allow me to introduce Josiah, Ruthie and Marie."

Bergen had risen to his feet—to the displeasure of Snowflake, who meowed loudly—and made a bow to the children. He then knelt down to greet the young girls of six and three. Ruthie was hiding behind Marie's skirts.

"I am very pleased to meet you, ladies."

"Why are you here, misther?" Marie asked.

"I brought your mama a donkey."

"That is a very thrange gift to bring her," Marie replied innocently.

"I suppose it is, but I was told she rescued animals and Clarence needed a home."

"Clarence is a very thrange name for a donkey," she continued, unperturbed.

"Oh, but there I must disagree. Once you meet him, you can see for yourself that he looks like a Clarence."

Marie furrowed her brow. "I do not know any Claranthes, so how will I know what they look like?" she protested.

Elizabeth was enjoying the look of consternation on Lord Bergen's face enormously and made no attempt to hush the girl. She wondered how quickly after dinner he would make his excuses and flee from the domesticity.

"I want to thee him," Marie pronounced and took Lord Bergen's hand to lead him outside.

"Perhaps after dinner," Elizabeth interrupted. "We do not wish to let the food go cold."

"It is already dark," Marie protested.

"Marie," Elizabeth said in a warning voice, "I promise there will be time to meet him later."

The butler announced dinner and Elizabeth ushered the children into the room behind Lord Bergen, who gallantly offered his arm to Aunt Jane. The vicar followed.

"Did I hear you say you brought a donkey?" Vicar Brown asked. He was bald as well as fat and appeared even less comely beside Lord Bergen's tall person.

"Indeed, you did," Bergen answered.

"It is surely God's providence. We need a donkey for the pageant to bring Mary into Bethlehem."

"I am not certain…" Bergen began to protest, but Elizabeth interrupted him.

"What an excellent idea!" Elizabeth declared. "You will fit on Clarence perfectly, Marie."

"I do not want to be Mary. I want to be a withe man," she protested.

"I do not wish to be Joseph and pretend to be married to my sister." Josiah finally spoke.

"Then perhaps we should not have a pageant this year," Aunt Jane remarked. "If the children do not wish to participate, then why do it at all?"

The vicar became flustered and sputtered, "Why, it is a tradition! We must tell the story of Christmas!"

"Then do it in your droll excuse for sermons from the pulpit!" Aunt Jane retorted.

"We will have the pageant, Vicar, never you fear," Elizabeth put in hastily. "It will all work out as it should, I am sure. Everyone, do, please, enjoy your dinner. We are simple folk here in the country, Lord Bergen. Three courses are enough for us, but I am sure it is not what you are used to."

"I prefer a good country meal, ma'am, to the current vogue for French cuisine. I appreciate your hospitality." He raised his glass in thanks and then served himself with some stuffed pigeon and boiled potatoes the footmen held before him.

Elizabeth frowned. She had expected dinner to be lively with the children present, but it was entirely too calm and comfortable.

The vicar was trying too hard to make Aunt Jane like him, as usual, and Ruthie was wearing more food than she was eating.

Lord Bergen was making an effort to speak to Josiah, who tended to shy away from men. Somehow, to her surprise, he was drawing more than one-word responses from the youth. In fact, the dinner felt shockingly normal and almost cosy—that is, until Marie's pet mouse, Nippy, decided to help himself to the cheese tray.

Lord Bergen maintained his composure, but the vicar jumped, spilling his wine into his lap.

"Good heavens!" he exclaimed, patting his napkin on his breeches as Aunt Jane laughed at him. The children quickly joined in. This was much more as expected, she thought, with a certain satisfaction.

"Forgive us, Vicar. Marie is not supposed to bring him in to dinner."

"She keeps a mouse for a pet?" he questioned.

"He is one of God'th creatureth, thir," Marie reprimanded, her lower lip protruding with disapproval.

"Perhaps it is time to go outside and meet the donkey," Aunt Jane suggested.

Ruthie was standing at the window and with a giggle, pointed at the glass.

"It appears Clarence has come to greet us," Lord Bergen said.

"He does not look like a donkey," Josiah remarked.

The vicar let out a deep sigh. "Perhaps we should cancel the pageant after all," he agreed as they all stood and looked at Clarence, who was beating his nose against the window pane.

Elizabeth opened the terrace door and Clarence jumped with apparent glee and began to make a noise.

"Is he trying to sing?" Aunt Jane asked, squinting into the dark.

"Did I not mention he is a singing donkey?" Bergen smiled.

"I like him, but I do not think I want to ride him. I want to be a withe man," Marie announced.

"And I do not want to be Joseph," Josiah stated.

"We have no one else to play Joseph," Elizabeth reminded him. "Perhaps Molly Satterley will play Mary instead."

"I do not wish to be Joseph!" Josiah said angrily, his face red.

"He likes Molly," Marie said innocently.

Josiah stomped off and Clarence began to howl.

"Hush, Clarence!" Lord Bergen commanded and surprisingly, the donkey obeyed.

"I am certain this is not what you are used to, Lord Bergen. Please do not feel the need to be polite and remain," Elizabeth suggested, trying not to laugh.

"Nonsense. This is far more entertaining than watching my best friend and his new wife make eyes at each other."

Elizabeth was not sure what to say to that. Lord Bergen had not been such a superficial cur as she had imagined him, and he had been good with the children. She suddenly felt exhausted and wanted this man to leave. The pageant was only a week away and now it seemed the whole idea was falling apart. She had wanted this Christmas to be special for the children.

"Did I say something wrong?" he asked.

"No, not at all. I am distracted by the pageant, sir. Forgive me."

"I will leave you, then," he said pleasantly.

Now Elizabeth felt like the cur here, but this was why she did not entertain notions of men and remarriage. She had no time for it.

"Thank you for Clarence. He will be a charming addition to our collection."

"Misther."

Elizabeth looked down to see Marie tugging on Lord Bergen's coat.

"Yes, Marie?" He knelt down to look her in the eye.

"I know how to make the pageant happen."

"How is that, Marie?"

"You be Joseph and Mama be Mary."

CHAPTER 3

*B*ergen would never have thought himself as a candidate for Joseph, as part of the Nativity. Taking a sideways glance at Lady Newton, he could tell she was equally startled by the pronouncement. It seemed so simple when little Marie suggested it. *Simple, yes, but a good idea? Maybe, maybe not.* When was the last time that he had really celebrated Christmas? He had gone to balls and done his share of flirting, delivered presents to the widows who struck his fancy, and generally accommodated the festivities to his own comfort. Yet here, in plain Stony Stratford, he had a widow, and was being considered as Joseph in a Christmas play. His friends would say this had the potential to be a much better Season than he had anticipated, even though this very attractive widow was already wearing what could be used as Mary's ancient dress—colour and all.

"Could I have another glass of wine, please?"

The vicar's request interrupted his thoughts.

"Certainly." Smiling, he passed the wine decanter to the elder cleric seated beside him.

"Marie, I am expected in London…" The look on her face stopped him in mid-sentence.

"Thir, Mama needs you to play Joseph because Josiah does not want to be Joseph and she loves the Christmas play."

Bergen could not resist Marie's plea. If Lady Newton were willing to do it, then he would, too.

"When exactly does the play take place?" He needed to get word to Aunt Faith that his plans had changed.

"It usually takes place on Christmas Eve, my lord. " The short, balding vicar reached across the dinner table and helped himself to another biscuit as he answered.

"Vicar, what animals could you consider using in the play?" Bergen asked. He was thinking of Clarence. The donkey seemed possessed of unexpected abilities. If it was to be a musical, surely Clarence could accompany the choir? *What am I about? A donkey singing in a musical pageant?* The thought made him laugh out loud. "I apologize. I did not mean to laugh. I was just thinking about Clarence and the many talents he seems to have."

"He will make a good donkey," Marie added.

"I trust you do not expect me to ride that little donkey!" Lady Newton exclaimed in astonishment.

Bergen bit back another deep laugh. *Now I would pay to see that.* "No, I would not think either of you would find that comfortable. I only asked because I wanted to know the vicar's thoughts on animals taking part in such entertainment.

"I do think we can use...ah...Clarence, is it?" The vicar finished blotting up the wine that was on his lap and refilled his glass.

"Help yourself, Vicar," shot Aunt Jane, her voice dripping with sarcasm. "You will find it is better than the grape juice you serve."

"Please, Vicar, pray tell me how you feel we can use Clarence on the stage?" Bergen hoped to smooth the rough pause created by Aunt Jane's acid words. He smothered a chuckle of appreciation. *The old termagant.*

The vicar took a large swig of red wine. "It *would* make things look authentic if we have the donkey on the stage. This little donkey seems rather rare. He sings, you say?" He chuckled. "Then he is rare, indeed!"

Bergen cleared his throat. "That is stating it mildly." He glanced at the window and was relieved that Clarence seemed to have settled down. He was not pawing or trying to gain attention. He seemed to be just...watching. If Bergen did not know better, he would swear the donkey was...listening. *No! Impossible.* Nevertheless, the feeling persisted. "Lady Newton, will you be participating as Mary, as little Marie suggested?" He hoped she would. Despite the drab gown she had chosen, he found her interesting, not to mention, beautiful. He was aware she was purposely trying to drive him away and for the life of him, he did not understand her motives.

Lady Newton had gone out of her way to make dinner difficult. He tried not to laugh, because it was having the reverse effect on him. She was wearing garments which indicated she was still in mourning, and she had included her three children—something that was normally frowned upon in Society. *Ha! A good chase makes the conquest that much better.* He had divested himself of his latest mistress because she had started whining and wanting too much of his time. He was not anxious to be leg-shackled and found widows to be a safer bet. Perhaps Lady Newton would ease his needs. He had hoped to find entertainment with the lovely Lady Burroughs, who was newly widowed and always made it known she was very anxious, but London would have to wait. Lady Newton would be a far more interesting diversion.

Dinner continued until the vicar stood up to leave. "I should be getting back to the vicarage." He looked at her aunt and nodded. "Aunt Jane, thank you for your delightful company. I always enjoy your spirited repartee. It keeps me on my toes, you know." The short, stocky man bubbled with laughter.

"Humph!" It was the first time in the evening the old woman was left without anything to say.

"Rehearsals for the play start tomorrow evening at five o'clock." He nodded to everyone and started to take his leave.

Bergen noted that the vicar had said 'start'. "What do you mean, Vicar, that rehearsals *start*? Surely there is not so much to learn?"

"Well, we always need a few rehearsals before everyone feels...er...

comfortable." The vicar looked a bit flustered at the question and looked to Lady Newton, who nodded.

"Yes, with the smaller children, it takes several practices for them to become comfortable with speaking in front of adults." Lady Newton answered and immediately rang the bell. The children's nurse appeared.

"Children, go with Miss Holly, please. I will be up directly." Elizabeth pushed back her chair and stood up. "Vicar, please let me walk you out. Thank you for coming. It was delightful."

The children pulled back from the table quietly and left the room without a word.

"Yes, indeed; most pleasant! Those are very well-behaved children. Yes, indeed; most well-behaved! I was glad to come. As always, your Aunt Jane—ah, the food, was delightful. If you do not mind me saying so, my lady, I think you and Lord Bergen would be wonderful in the pageant. Providing we do not have you ride the donkey, Lady Newton, might we count on your participation?"

"Very well, if you insist." Elizabeth's voice was barely above a whisper.

"Very good!" The vicar was all smiles and rubbed his abdomen in a circular motion with one hand. "The children can be the wise men, and, ah, Clarence can participate as well." Patting his stomach, the vicar grabbed his hat and coat and made his way out into the evening.

"I am not sure how the plan has changed so drastically, but since it is a Christmas pageant, I suppose I will do it," remarked Lady Newton. "Please do not feel obligated, my lord."

"I would very much like to participate, if you are amenable." Bergen smiled in earnest. "I shall be honoured to be Joseph."

Elizabeth rubbed her temple but did not reply.

"I will also take my leave, Lady Newton," he continued. "You appear tired. I do have one lingering question, however. How often will there need to be a rehearsal?" He envisioned rehearsing a time or two and then coming back a day or so before Christmas.

"We practice every other day until the pageant—starting tomorrow. "That will give us four rehearsals," Elizabeth responded, smiling sweetly.

Bergen and the two women made their way into the hall, where the butler had his coat, gloves and hat ready. "I should make arrangements." He sketched a bow and the butler opened the door. "Until tomorrow, my lady."

Elizabeth smiled with genuine amusement. "It appears that way, my lord. We will have dinner at five o'clock and then leave for the church afterwards. You are more than welcome to join us for dinner."

When Bergen returned to the inn, he found his room was still available. Before he settled down for the night, he wrote his aunt a quick missive and gave it to Perry to post for him in the morning. He decided to have a night-cap and took a glass of ale upstairs. As he turned from closing the door, he noticed the glow of a camp-fire behind the hotel. How likely would it be that the same people were still camped behind his room? He pulled up the window and blew out his light. *I should be ashamed of myself*, he thought, *but I am starving for entertainment.* He sipped the ale he had brought up with him and waited. After a few moments, he heard a familiar voice engaged in conversation, an argument in the starlight which brought his attention.

"I don't know what happened to the donkey. I tied him up and he was gone when I went back to look for the amulet." The familiar voice sounded angry.

"You should have taken the amulet before you dumped the beast. It could have brought luck. You need to find it. It could bring good fortune." The second man's voice was deep. The two men—dark figures in the flickering gloom—kicked at the already waning camp-fire to put it out and then walked into two separate tents.

Bergen closed his window. "That did not last long." He scratched his head. "I wonder what they want with the little donkey's collar amulet. It is just a blue stone." Maybe it was something he should look at more closely. It had been a long day, one that was surely leading to an even more fascinating day tomorrow. He at once felt guilty for putting off Aunt Faith. He had promised to be there by now.

ELIZABETH SHUT the door behind Lord Bergen and leaned her head against it. Life was exhausting and she did not need this complication. Lord Bergen had surprised her, though. He had not seemed at all discouraged or annoyed with the children. Perhaps she had wronged him. However, he was too handsome and charming—could he truly mean to stay for the pageant? It did not seem real.

Her husband had been handsome and charming in the beginning, too, and she had learned her lesson well. Now she was left to bring up his bastard children, he and their mother having been killed in a fire. There really had been no other choice but to take the children to raise as her own. They were precious, and it was no fault of theirs that their father had been living a double life. Mistresses were accepted amongst the *ton*—their bastards were not.

Slowly, she climbed the stairs to the nursery to kiss the children good night. Ruthie and Marie were already asleep, snuggled together. Josiah was sitting on his bed, fingering something blue.

"What have you there?" she asked as she sat on the edge of his mattress and placed an arm around him. At first, he covered the item, as though to hide it; then he held it out to her.

"I found it around the donkey's neck."

"Oh. May I see?" She turned over the blue stone and examined the pinkish purple star-shower in the centre. There was a glimmer which seemed to come from behind the star. It was pretty, although probably the most unusual design she had ever seen.

"Do you think it is beautiful?" Josiah asked. "I wonder why he was wearing it."

"That is a good question. I believe amulets are thought by the gypsies to hold special powers. Perhaps they placed it on him."

"I would not have left it—or him. I bet Clarence is really sad. It does not feel good to be left behind."

Elizabeth hugged Josiah close. "No, it does not; but he has a good home now, as you do. I know I cannot replace your real mama, but you will always be safe and cared for here."

"I know. I did not mean to say you are not a good mama. I am grateful to you."

"I know I will never replace your real parents. I understand that."

Elizabeth handed the amulet back to the boy and he fingered it while she hugged him and wished him good night.

"Lizzie?" he asked as she walked away. She turned back at the query in his tone.

"The fancy lord likes you."

"I would not worry about him. He will be gone after the pageant."

"I liked him. He treated me as a real person."

"I am glad. He was very kind. You must not think yourself anything other than a real person, though, my dear." She smiled and closed the door behind her yet could not help worrying as she hurried to her room. What was that confounded man up to?

"Stop it, Lizzie!" she chastised herself. "You are reading far too much into this," she muttered as she closed the door behind her.

"What was that, my lady?" Hannah asked.

"I fear I'm talking to myself, Hannah." She allowed the maid to unlace her, and then sat at the dressing table to take her hair down.

"The word downstairs is that the London Lord is downright handsome. I wish I'd had a chance to see him."

"I suppose he is, but handsome is as handsome does," she replied, though she immediately felt guilty for being so harsh. In truth, Lord Bergen had done nothing wrong.

"Well, they say he was very kind to his horse and not at all high and mighty with the grooms or footmen," Hannah added as she brushed Elizabeth's hair. Elizabeth closed her eyes and relaxed at the soothing motion.

"That only means he gave them handsome vails," she retorted.

CHAPTER 4

"*W*hat is *this?*" The short woman with greying hair swatted her mahogany writing desk and huffed her displeasure, speaking to anyone within earshot of the room. The slap on her desk upset a small, open bottle of ink, causing it to rock and then, fall from the desk to the rug below, spilling. "My nephew is known for his good humour and his good times, the rogue, but I will not allow him to be taken in by her." The old woman laid her nephew's letter down and rang for her butler. Unable to sit still, she paced across the room to her new acquisition, a blue and gold linen-covered settee, and straightened the rolled side pillows. Snatching the note up from the desk, she gripped the brass dog's head handle on her cane and sat down on the small couch, softly thumping the cane on the floor in an effort to contain her displeasure.

A few moments later, a tall, thin man appeared. He had a balding pate and thick patches of slightly greying hair on the sides of his head.

"Winston. I find myself having to rescue my nephew, Lord Bergen, and I may not have a moment to lose." She slapped the missive against the mahogany frame of the sofa in a pique of irritation and opened it up again to read it. Muttering, she looked at the name of the town her nephew had mentioned. "I do not recognize that town. However, there cannot be two with the same name. I will not allow my brother's child to have that woman sink her claws into him. When did she move there? I thought she was in London. Well, no matter. She has had two husbands already and led countless decent men into financial ruin. My nephew will not be her newest conquest." She huffed again. "Winston, have Alice attend me."

"Very good, my lady." With a bow, the wizened man left the room.

Leaning on her cane, Lady Faith Bergen stood up, unable to continue sitting, and fidgeted around the parlour, fuming, until her maid arrived.

"Alice, pack my trunks, if you please," she ordered the girl. "I find that I need to rescue my nephew."

"Lord Bergen, my lady? Are you not expecting him for the Christmastide season?"

"Drat! He was supposed to be here two days hence, but along the way he met a widow, and not just *any* widow. His letter says he met a… I think it says *Mrs.* Newton. The ink blurred next to her name. Anyway, somehow, he has allowed this widow to convince him to stay…in Stony Stratford, of all places." Lady Faith declared her displeasure with her voice raised so high, she squeaked as she finished her account.

"My lady…your voice. You know what the doctor has told you about getting so excited."

"Yes, yes, you are right, Alice." She shook her head and gently caressed her neck. "I must not lose my voice. I have a lot to say when I see that lad!"

"I have never been to Stony Stratford, my lady. Is it a big town? Will we be staying, my lady?"

"I confess I have not been there either. I have heard of it, of course." She drew herself up and pursed her lips. "I am afraid we will have to stay for at least a day or so. It falls upon me to rescue my nephew from this unscrupulous woman. Please dispatch a groom to make arrangements for us at a posting inn. Let me see what the letter says." She shook open the half-beaten missive.

"Bergen mentions an inn called The Cock. It must be one of the places where he regularly stays...but no matter, that helps. Let the groom know I expect the very best accommodations and we may be there for one or two nights. And please find someone to clean up the spill I just made in my fit of displeasure." She nodded at the spilled ink.

"Yes, my lady." Alice curtsied and left to do her mistress's bidding.

Meanwhile, Lady Bergen sat down at her desk and took out a piece of vellum.

"He has friends also expecting him. I suppose it would not hurt to enlist their aid," she muttered to herself. Although in a hurry, she decided to pen a quick note to his friend, the Earl of Shefford and let him know of Bergen's delay and her determination to rescue him.

BERGEN THOUGHT Lady Newton had seemed somewhat introspective towards the end of play practice this evening. Maybe it was a signal he was making some headway. Her children were delightful, especially little Marie. Ah, but she was a caring one. Laughing aloud, he considered what was keeping him here. A Christmas pageant, of all things; it was quite ridiculous. He wished he could turn back time, just to see again Lady Newton's face when Marie suggested her mother be Mary and he be Joseph. He was certain he had heard her gasp, and each time he gave thought to it, he laughed. Nonetheless, staying for the play was significantly delaying his journey to London, and his friends would be looking for him.

The warm sun had traded places with a full moon and a frigid wind when he and Merry were approaching the same turn where, earlier in the day, he could have sworn he heard voices. He recalled hearing both a male and female voice behind the mulberry bush Clarence had been tied to only yesterday, but now could see no one on the road from his vantage point. On this return trip to Stony Stratford, he stilled to listen. There was nothing. He and his horse rode quietly on, without voices or interruptions, until he pulled up at The Cock.

"You are back, my lord!" Perry was excited and clearly happy to see him, nearly running forward to help him with Merry. "Welcome back! It is beef pie tonight. It be my favourite meal. I hope there will be some worthy scraps."

"Do you get the scraps?" Bergen asked.

"Not every night, my lord. If we are busy, we only get the uneaten bread. But that satisfies." The young lad smiled and pocketed the three shillings Bergen gave him before leading Merry to the stables. "I will take good care of her, my lord," he said, turning around.

"Thank you, Perry. It appears I will be here for a few more days."

"Yes, my lord." The boy nodded as he spoke. "We have just received word of important visitors coming from London. 'Tis a mighty important lady who be coming to our small town. Everyone is having to clean the inn from top to bottom."

"That is interesting news, Perry. I shall be curious to see who arrives."

Bergen tried to think of a lady he could know who would be making a trip to this country town at this time of year. No one came to mind. Dismissing it, he let himself inside. The inn was busy with its normal rowdy customers, but Bergen saw that a huge door he had not previously noticed, which gave access to the tap-room, had been closed in an effort to control some of the noise. The innkeeper and his wife were scurrying about issuing orders to their minions. The advanced notice of the expected entourage seemed to have set them by the ears.

"Good evening, my lord. Welcome back. We had not expected you but are very glad of your return." The innkeeper was breathing hard from exertion. "Will you be wanting your room again tonight?"

"Yes. I realize I should have mention this last evening when I returned, but I believe I will be staying for a few more days. I will eat in the dining room tonight, if the kitchen is still serving." Dinner had been extraordinary, and with all of the excitement, he had not eaten much of it. A light repast, he thought, would allow for a better night's sleep.

"Very good, my lord." The innkeeper sent a maid to check the bedchamber had been prepared and directed Bergen to the dining room. "Right this way, my lord."

Bergen looked about in amazement. The room was clean. Surfaces were sparkling. Every table had either two opposing chairs, or four neatly placed around it. Mats, utensils, napkins and a small vase of wild flowers graced each table. A fire roared in the huge stone fireplace, which had been cleaned of the usual smut and grime. He wished his friend Edward, the Earl of Weston, could see this room. He would not recognize it as the same inn they had frequented on their trips to London, and where they had raised so much revelry.

Chuckling to himself, Bergen sat down and ordered a mug of ale and a beef pie—recognizing he was hungrier than he thought. The vicar had seemed to be the only one truly enjoying the dinner they had, once again, all shared at Newton Grange. He thought again of Lady Newton's children and realized he did not want to disappoint them. Josiah's face flashed through his mind. *I wonder what it is that causes the boy such unrest. He has happy surroundings, so there must be something troubling him from before.* Bergen thought of his own childhood and his parents, both now gone. They had always laughed a lot together. He could not remember a time when he had been maudlin while growing up—until he had lost his parents when still young. Boxing Day and Christmastide had always been a joyful time for his family, and yet he now barely celebrated it, except quietly with Aunt Faith. Tomorrow he would go to town and buy gifts for the children, hoping Lady Newton would find it acceptable.

"Your pie and ale, my lord." He looked up and had difficulty clamping his mouth shut from the shock of the vision in front of him. The buxom maid who had brought his food was scarce recognizable as the same tavern wench who served ale and behaved loosely with customers. Tonight, her hair was hidden under a tidy mob-cap and she wore a high-collared, brown gown which gave no sneak view of the endowments usually on display. The dress even appeared cleaned and pressed. A pity, he thought, as he sipped his ale and attacked his pie.

ELIZABETH HAD NOT SEEN or heard from Lord Bergen since rehearsal and dinner the day before, and she was beginning to think she had imagined the whole episode. As she dressed for this evening's pageant rehearsal, she decided she would not put on any more displays to give him a disgust of her. People in the town would begin to talk and wonder why she was behaving so oddly.

"That's more like it, my lady," Hannah remarked when she saw that Elizabeth had chosen a more flattering gown the colour of jade.

"I decided I could not concern myself with Lord Bergen...should he even return today."

"Oh, he is still here, all right and tight." Elizabeth smiled inwardly at the maid's use of a phrase more commonly employed in the stables. "So, it seems, is some other fancy London lady. There is a lot of talk downstairs. Sally's brother works at the Cock and told her all about it."

"Why should our quiet town suddenly have all these visitors during Christmastide?"

"I could not say, my lady, but it is my belief Lord Bergen has his eye on you and he will nay leave afore he's been told you ain't having none." Her voice rose and her careful speech lost its precision with her excitement.

"That is quite enough of that, Hannah."

The maid looked unrepentant. "Yes, my lady. I do think as he'd be right delicious like your Aunt Jane says." She hurried from the room before Elizabeth could retort.

Turning to the looking-glass, Elizabeth let out a deep sigh. She was only six and twenty, but she felt much older. Studying her image in the mirror, she reflected that she was in better looks than at the end, when Horace had treated her so poorly. Much of the strain of that time was beginning to fade and there was some bloom to her cheeks again. She stood and examined her reflection. While she was a little fuller than she had been as a bride of eighteen, when she had married, she thought her figure was not yet to be deplored. Pressing her stomach to settle the butterflies swirling inside, she shook her head and left her chamber.

"Silly, silly girl," she chastised herself. "He is only interested in his own amusement."

Dinner seemed different without Bergen this night. Elizabeth had to admit to herself that she missed his company at the table and found herself looking forward to pageant practice this evening. The children were waiting for her, already bundled up in warm clothes, to go to the church. She put on her own cape, hat and muff, and followed the little party outside into the cold December night. The groom was holding Clarence ready and the donkey jounced around with obvious glee when he saw them.

"Are you ready to go, little fellow?" Elizabeth asked. He nodded his head as though he understood her. "Josiah, you lead him," she instructed.

They walked up Mill Lane and Elizabeth could not but enjoy the smell of wood-burning in the chimneys and the frost covering the grass.

"Burr! I think we might have a white Christmas," Elizabeth said. "We will have to make the church look like a stable instead of holding it outside."

"I like snow," Ruthie said.

"I like Chrithmath," Marie said. "Cook thaith we can help make thome thweeth."

Ruthie nodded agreement.

"Dried fruits are one of my favourite parts about this season," Elizabeth agreed, "but food and gifts are not what Christmas is about."

"Baby Jesus," little Ruthie said around the thumb in her mouth.

"I don't see what the fuss is all about!" Josiah said and then covered his mouth. "I am sorry, Lizzie. I did not mean to say that aloud."

Josiah was the one who remembered his mother best since he was the eldest at eleven, which was why he still called Elizabeth by her given name, much though it was frowned upon by the dowagers of the neighbourhood.

"I think it is normal to question what Christmas is all about," she said carefully. "Sometimes it is hard to understand why we celebrate the birth of a baby born hundreds of years ago."

The children had lost their mother the previous year, at the festive season, and Elizabeth did not know if they had been included in the Christmas celebrations. She doubted it very much, for in most gently bred households it was deemed an adult festivity. Having always disagreed with this fashionable custom, she wanted to make her own Christmas traditions and ensure this Feast of Stephen was special for all of them. Hopefully, Lord Bergen would not ruin it.

"Maybe you will understand better after the pageant," she said to Josiah. He shrugged his shoulders and looked away. "Why do you not leave Clarence in the stable at the vicarage until we are ready for him? I doubt very much that he is trained to be indoors," Elizabeth said with a smile. Clarence smiled back at her and shook his head as though in answer. The children laughed, Josiah included.

They entered the church and Elizabeth's heart began to race when she saw Lord Bergen standing at the altar with the vicar, holding a baby. Even her womb turned over at the sight of him with a child and she cursed her body's reaction to him. Then she felt guilty for cursing, even under her breath, inside a church.

"Ah, there is the star of the pageant!" the vicar said in greeting.

Elizabeth and the girls walked down the aisle. "I think the baby Jesus is the star," she corrected.

"No, the thar is up there," Marie pointed to the star which had been hung on the ceiling.

"I see you have already decided to move the pageant indoors," Elizabeth noted, looking around the nave.

"Yes, yes. It is much too cold," Vicar Brown agreed.

Lord Bergen left the altar and handed the baby back to its mother, a local seamstress, who was sitting in the front pew. He knelt down to look Marie in the eye.

"You are correct, but I think your mama meant that the baby is the most special part."

"Oh." She thought about this for a moment and then nodded. "Yeth he ith."

"Shall we take our places?" the vicar asked. "Wise men stand over here…" He pointed to the left side. "…and stay back until after the baby is born. Mrs. Groom will play a song and I will read the Christmas story from Luke."

"Joseph will walk Mary down the aisle with the donkey and kneel before the manger."

Lord Bergen had taken her arm to lead her to the rear of the church and Elizabeth shivered. This was getting out of hand!

"The needth a baby in her middle!" Marie insisted loudly, and Elizabeth could have died where she was, at that very moment.

Elizabeth turned back to the front of the church and noted that the vicar's cheeks were quite red. She could not look at Lord Bergen for fear of what he might say. Then he leaned near to her and whispered in her ear:

"Marie is a very wise girl."

Elizabeth took a deep breath, ignoring the connotations of his words. It was a very sore point in her chest for Elizabeth, not having been blessed with a child, and she wanted one of her own so very badly.

Marie was being consoled by Aunt Jane, who was explaining that they would use a pillow to make it look as though Mary was about to have a baby and then they would remove it after they arrived at the manger.

Marie was frowning and did not seem satisfied. Elizabeth was praying silently that the child would not continue. She did not wish to have this discussion in front of anyone, let alone Lord Bergen, who was still standing too close. She should move away, but his size and warmth were somehow comforting while also unsettling.

"Why are you frowning?" he asked.

She gazed up into his blue eyes; all at once it was hard to find words. She turned away so she could think.

"I-I was just wondering how to deal with Marie."

"It looks as if Aunt Jane has taken care of the problem for you. Shall we?"

Elizabeth looked up, and sure enough, the three youngsters were happily holding their gifts of 'gold', 'frankincense' and 'myrrh', and looking at them expectantly.

"And Joseph also went up from Galilee, out of the city of Nazareth, into Judaea, unto the city of David, which is called Bethlehem, to be taxed with Mary his espoused wife, being great with child. And so, it was, that while they were there, the days were accomplished that she should be delivered."

Bergen led Elizabeth down the aisle. "Is Clarence not to rehearse with us?" he asked.

"Oh! We left him in the stables."

"We can rehearse the play once more with him."

"I think that would be a good idea."

As they reached the front and knelt behind the manger, Aunt Jane came hustling in with a pillow.

"What are you doing, woman?" the vicar asked, his voice raised.

"Are you so stupid you have to ask? Did you not hear Marie insisting on Mary being with child?"

The vicar looked to the statue of Christ in exasperation. Elizabeth stared at him with widened eyes, fearing what was coming next. Fore-stalling any further argument from Aunt Jane or prosing from the vicar, she filled the sudden silence.

"We will practice again with Clarence and I will pretend to be with child," she said sharply.

"No, we mutht do it properly, like the Bible thayth."

Josiah ran out to fetch Clarence, while Elizabeth clenched her teeth. She wanted nothing more than to run outside herself and go home.

Lord Bergen was too close; he whispered in her ear again. "All will be well. There is no harm in doing it properly."

Elizabeth needed a glass of wine. Instead, Lord Bergen practically lifted her up and ushered her off into an ante-room so she might stuff a pillow under her dress. Why, oh why, had she thought she could take this part?

"Shall I help you with that?" Lord Bergen asked. There was a wicked gleam in his eyes.

Elizabeth slammed the door in his face and wondered how she was supposed to hold a pillow under her dress and it not fall out but be accessible to remove behind the manger.

"Who would have thought the Christmas story would be so complicated?" she asked herself before walking awkwardly back into the nave.

"You look splendid with child," Bergen said in response to her reappearance. He was waiting just outside the door.

"Let us have this over with," she muttered.

Bergen helped her to hold the pillow in place with the arm he was guiding her with, and she refrained from reprimanding him, because she could not have done it otherwise. Clarence pranced with glee when he saw him, and Elizabeth was afraid the whole pageant would become a farce.

"Take your places, everyone!" the vicar shouted. The music began softly, and the vicar read the passage again.

After they knelt behind the manger, Bergen lifted her skirt and discreetly pulled the pillow out. Elizabeth tried to keep her thoughts pure, but unfortunately, when his hand brushed her leg, other thoughts pervaded. The vicar was reading, and the baby was brought from somewhere and was placed in her arms. Liz Elizabeth wanted to cry as she laid him in the manger.

Then Bergen's arm wrapped around her again. To her astonishment, he seemed completely unaffected by the whole scene.

The children came before the manger and presented their gifts. Elizabeth tried to smile at them and nodded her head in encouragement, but she wanted the rehearsal to be over—and she needed to be far away from Lord Bergen. She had to find a way to resist his charms.

CHAPTER 5

"What an odd adornment for an animal!" The vicar wiped sweat away from over his eyes as he rolled the blue amulet over and over in his hands. Clarence stood still, his gaze intent on the old vicar's face.

Bergen could see what appeared to be some attachment to the piece of jewellery from the donkey. For now, he and Elizabeth had agreed it might be better if Clarence not wear it, in the event that it be seen by the gypsy Bergen had heard discussing the animal's whereabouts.

"And you say young Josiah is keeping this for safekeeping for the donkey?" The vicar talked as he continued to examine the stone.

The donkey nodded and Bergen laughed. He would swear the donkey understood what was being discussed. Vicar Brown wanted to meet before the final play rehearsal and the room was extremely warm. The odd foursome—the vicar, Bergen, Elizabeth and Clarence—stood inside the church office while the children were at the altar with the church curate and a lady volunteering from the village, reviewing the previous night's practice.

"Yes. There is rather more to the story than you may have supposed. I am afraid he came with it. And I agree, Vicar; we felt it was an odd piece, as well. In fact, it seems to have created a bit of a problem for Clarence, as his previous owners felt he was cursed. His previous owner belonged to a troupe of gypsies who happened to be camped not far from the Cock Inn. My room overlooked the encampment and it was not difficult to overhear their discussion. It is my fear that, after abandoning the poor animal, they may be interested in his collar." Bergen watched the vicar's reaction, carefully, curious as to the cleric's thoughts of the odd jewel.

"You have certainly had an interesting stay at the inn, my lord." He chortled and then cleared his throat. "I believe it is owned by two of our long-standing parishioners. I will mention you to them, if that would be acceptable. They are most supportive of our little church."

"Certainly. The story behind our acquiring Clarence is most unusual, and I would like your insight on it. First, do you mind if I open the window just a bit?" Bergen did not wait to have an answer before he pulled up on the casement and opened the window. Clarence was behaving himself, but he already knew the animal well enough to know fresh air could become necessary at any moment.

"Yes, yes. Pray, go on." The vicar steadied himself against the corner of his desk and tilted his head to show he was listening.

Bergen continued, "I was retiring for the night and had a window open slightly to allow some fresh air into the room." Observing the vicar's frown, he said apologetically, "I find I cannot sleep without. The dormitory at school was exceeding cold; I expect that is why. Anyway, to proceed with the tale. The gypsies were rather loud, and their voices carried into my room on the late-evening breeze." Not for a king's ransom would he admit to sitting beneath the window and listening like a common eavesdropper. Still, he was interested in what the vicar might know.

"He appears to be such a young donkey, but curiously, calm." The older man laid the donkey's amulet down and searched out a book from a small wooden bookshelf which sat on the opposite corner of the worn oak desk from where he perched. "Ah! Here it is." He waved the small brown book, opened at a page. "I thought I recalled seeing this. It has to do with the colour of the stone and the shape in the

middle of the blue stone. Let me read you what it says. Ah…here it is."
His fat forefinger followed the text as he read it.

> *Those of whom a blue star-beam hears*
> *Shalt know but the truth spok'n to their ears*
> *And should the stone ornament a yoke,*
> *So, the wearer shall follow all that be spoke...*
> *What then be said hold true and sincere,*
> *Forever, Amen, throughout the years.*

"CLARENCE, you appear to be an object of truth!" Bergen burst into laughter, joined by Elizabeth. "No wonder the troupe thought the animal cursed. I recall they spoke of horse-dealing that had not exactly been successful." He reached over and stroked Clarence behind the ears. "It is perfect that you will be the donkey for this Christmas play, little man." The little donkey bared his clenched teeth and nodded, appearing to smile. "I believe you are understanding what we say, after all. I am not sure that is always wise, you know, sir." Bergen laughed.

"How odd you should say that, my lord. Sometimes the truth can be a curse in itself." The old vicar appeared to consider this information. "And I should add that the curse extends to anyone possessing the collar, and at the moment, that would be young Josiah." As though forgetting their presence, the vicar rambled on, "Children rarely lie, anyway."

"I would infinitely prefer my children to speak only the truth to me, so Clarence is a welcome addition to my family." Elizabeth smiled and clasped her hands.

"Clarence is a lucky animal to have found a home with such care for his comfort and safety," the vicar answered.

"Thank you for the information on the amulet. It throws a new light on the matter." Bergen turned to Elizabeth. "I am afraid I have complicated things for you, Lady Newton. If these gypsies come for

Clarence, please consider turning over the amulet. It is what they want."

"I would *never* turn over poor Clarence." Elizabeth stroked the donkey's head. "The travelling troupe has already abandoned this poor animal once. I cannot abide abuse of any animal. As far as I am concerned, they can have the amulet if they want it." She picked up the stone and dropped it into the pocket of her gown. "Perhaps we should leave the rehearsal this evening. The children should go to bed soon."

Bergen watched the woman next to him as she stroked the head of the donkey in her care. She was exactly what he had imagined his countess would be—warm, generous of heart, a good mother, strong of temperament, resourceful—all qualities he wanted, but only when he was ready to have a countess. Yet if he was not ready to be leg-shackled, why was he still here? There were children to consider. Clearly, Elizabeth was not the type of woman with whom he could dally with and then leave. Suddenly, he realized the answer. He wanted to see how this friendship could unfold. He had never met anyone quite like her. She was not coy—she was anything but that. Elizabeth was not pretentious. He actually enjoyed talking with her—unlike the vapid widows he normally dawdled with, or the young débutantes his Aunt Faith paraded in front of him, a circumstance which forced him to limit his visits to Christmastide. He discovered, to his surprise, he wanted Elizabeth, and for once his interest was for all the right reasons. Contented with his resolve, he smiled at the woman walking next to him. He loved a good pursuit.

COLIN NELSON, the fifth Earl of Shefford, read and reread an urgent missive from Lady Faith Bergen. He shook his head and chuckled. It was apparent that her well-meaning rescue would come as a shock to his very good friend, Bergen. Added to that, the woman she was referring to, the *notorious* Mrs. Newton, lived here in London. He was not sure with whom Bergen was dallying, but he felt sure that his best friend would be shocked when his aunt arrived to rescue him. Colin imagined the confrontation that could occur between Bergen and his mettlesome aunt and nearly doubled over with laughter. *I am not going to miss that!* He slapped his leg and laughed harder. Bergen and Weston had always joined him at this time of year, and the three of them celebrated the year-end with whatever London amusements fulfilled their needs. Weston had recently married, so his holiday would be decidedly different, but he and Bergen had planned to carry on their traditions. Their amusements were relatively tame—a widow here and there, sparring at Gentleman Jackson's with old friends and, at times, a little gambling. Shefford automatically justified their peccadilloes as he recounted their fun to himself.

He had always spent Christmas with his mother, who still shared the family town house—now his since his father's recent death—and Bergen always visited his aunt. They both counted dodging her staid social events among their annual activities. It was apparent his friend had begun his celebrating early and if there was to be a rescue, Shefford would not want to miss the fireworks. That in itself would be very diverting. Shefford laughed harder as he imagined the supposed rescue and rang for his butler.

A middle-aged, balding man appeared. "Yes, my lord? How can I be of assistance?"

Shefford cleared his throat and brought the chair back in to an upright posture and removed his feet from their careless resting position on the corner of his desk.

"Franklin, I have received an interesting missive. I should like to discuss it with my mother. Is she at home?"

"Yes, my lord. Lady Shefford arrived home about a half-hour ago."

"Wonderful. Would you ask her to join me for a few moments? And ask Joseph to pack a small travelling satchel for me. I find that I am heading to Stony Stratford for a day or so. Please have my horse readied." He slapped the missive on his knee and looked up, still smiling.

"Will that be all, my lord?"

"Yes, Franklin."

"Very good, my lord." The butler bowed and withdrew.

A short time later, Lady Amelia Shefford glided elegantly into the room. At six-and-forty, she was still a very attractive woman, and wore her light brown hair in a softly curled style, pulled away from her still youthful face.

"My son, I thought you and your friend Bergen would have been at Gentleman Jim's by now. Is that not the first place you go when he arrives?" Her soft smile let him know she was gently prodding him. He enjoyed his mother's humour and respected her opinion on many matters.

He smiled at her gibe. "*Gentleman Jackson's*, Mother. And it is curious that you mention that because Bergen seems to have run into a slight...diversion on his way to London. It seems that he stopped in Stony Stratford and met a *Mrs. Newton...*" He paused for effect. "...who has convinced him to stay long enough to participate in a Christmas pageant. His Aunt Faith found out—probably from a note written by Bergen explaining his delay—and wrote to make me aware of her plan to rescue him from what she believes is his ruination."

"Surely that cannot be *the* Mrs. Newton? She is in London as we speak. While we do not move in the same circles, I know this to be true." She smiled broadly at her son. "Oh, goodness! His aunt is a colourful woman, indeed."

"I will not ask how you know of Mrs. Newton." He grinned at his mother. "But I am certain that Bergen will not be expecting his aunt. I plan to leave immediately." Shefford was always amused at his mother's polite candour.

"Yes, I believe her appearance might add a spark of...something... to his friendship with *Lady* Newton. I believe she is the widow of Lord Horace Newton, and she is a very proper lady. Lady Newton will be shocked to have been confused with a woman of such questionable...values, I am sure." She cleared her throat.

"I must leave immediately, Mother. Your information has helped immensely."

"Did Bergen's aunt happen to mention what part he was playing in the pageant?" Her lips were tightly closed on the question, but amusement was shining in her eyes.

"No, but somehow I doubt his role is one of the wise men." Grinning, he leaned over and kissed his mother goodbye. *Bergen, what in the world have you got yourself into this time?*

LORD BERGEN INSISTED on walking Elizabeth home from the church. The children had left earlier with Aunt Jane and she had stayed behind to speak with the vicar. Lord Bergen seemed to be everywhere, and she simply could not fathom why he found anything to interest him in helping with the pageant. He must have dozens of women fawning over him in London, so surely, he could not be staying just for her?

"What are you thinking?" Lord Bergen asked as he walked along beside her, his arms clasped behind his back. He was very handsome, and a younger Elizabeth would have been enamoured with the possibilities of being Lady Bergen.

"I was wondering why you are still here," she blurted out. Immediately, she clasped her hand over her mouth.

Lord Bergen laughed. "That was certainly plain speaking."

"I suppose it is the truth," she answered, gasping as the reason for her damning words occurred to her. "The amulet!"

Lord Bergen smiled and then his lips broadened into that boyishly wicked grin. "So, I can ask you anything now and you will have to answer honestly."

Elizabeth pulled the amulet from her pocket and attempted to drop it into the front pocket of his greatcoat. He grabbed her wrist and pulled her close, wrapping his hand around hers with the amulet still inside.

His face was so close to hers, she could feel his breath upon her mixed with a hint of sandalwood. He tilted her chin upwards to look into his eyes. Even she knew she was in deep trouble. Many a stronger woman would fall hard under his spell.

"Please do not," she whispered.

"But I must know," he pleaded.

"Why? I have no doubt you have women lining up in London for your pleasure. Why come here and insert yourself, not only into my life, but into the children's also? You will leave again in a few days. It is not fair to them."

"And what about you, Elizabeth? What would it do to you? Would you care if I left? Or do you want me to stay?"

Elizabeth tried to lie, but she could not say it. She pressed her lips together, but the amulet betrayed her. To avoid his knowing gaze, she turned her face away.

"Say it, Elizabeth."

"Yes. Yes, I want you to stay."

Bergen smiled, and she was lost. His lips descended on hers, and a wave of pleasure such as she had never felt before rushed through her body. His hands reached up to cradle her face with a tenderness she had never experienced. Horace had barely kissed her with a brief touch on the lips, and now Lord Bergen was teasing them open with his tongue. Elizabeth did not want to think of Horace, and she melted into Lord Bergen's body. His arms came around her and pulled her close, and his hands began to caress her back and bottom. Good Lord! He was caressing her bottom in public! She pulled back, her chest heaving, and looked around. It was dark, and no one was about.

"Goodness! We got carried away," she exclaimed.

"It was wonderful, was it not?" he answered. By the bright moonlight, she saw he was still grinning at her.

"Yes," she admitted unwillingly.

He pulled her behind a tree and kissed her again. This time, it was harder, more passionate.

"I love this amulet," he said as he showered kisses upon her neck and downward. He loosened some of her laces and rubbed his hand over one of her breasts.

"Do you like that?" he asked.

"Yes, damn you!" she replied, squirming. "But we cannot do this, Bergen," she said, though her nether regions were screaming otherwise.

"Why not? I like it; you seem to like it. What is the harm in enjoying each other?"

Elizabeth was finding it harder and harder to answer that question. She had never felt pleasure like this. In that moment, she wanted to be lost in it. Her back was now up against the tree. When had that happened? She felt his hand slide her dress upwards, and between her legs she was throbbing.

"Do you want more?"

"Why are you talking?" she demanded—with difficulty, for she had her head thrown back and was trying to hold in a groan.

He laughed wickedly and went down on his knees as he pulled her skirts up.

"What are you doing to my mama, thir?" Elizabeth heard Marie's voice ask the question.

Oh, God, no. Please no. Elizabeth was mortified. *Please do not let her have seen anything.*

"Your mama stepped on something. I was just checking her leg." Bergen had risen quickly and pulled her skirts down. Elizabeth was trying to think straight, but her senses were muddled.

"Ith Mama all right?" the little girl asked.

No, Mama was not all right.

"Yes, yes she will be quite well in a moment."

"Then you had better come inside out of the cold," Marie insisted and took his hand.

"I think you are right," Bergen answered as they walked away. "What are you doing out here alone?"

"I brought Clarence a carrot from the kitchen. He wanted one."

"He did, did he?"

Elizabeth opened her eyes to see Marie leading Lord Bergen back to the house. She looked down; the stupid amulet was still in her hand.

She took a moment to compose herself and then went to make sure Clarence was comfortable. She had not even realized they had walked back to the estate.

"Clarence, what have I done?"

He made a strange noise that sounded like, "I don't know."

Elizabeth shook her head. Her world had been turned upside down, and instead of wishing Lord Bergen to the devil, she only wished he could finish what he started. She was about to tie the amulet back around the donkey's neck when she heard a noise behind her. Quickly, she slipped it back in her pocket and ran into the house.

"Where have you been?" Aunt Jane asked with a sly, knowing look on her face as she stood in the hallway.

"I was visiting Clarence." Thank goodness she could answer truthfully.

"Well, come on in and warm yourself by the fire. There is some wassail as well."

"That sounds lovely," Elizabeth agreed. When she entered the drawing room, however, she was arrested by the sight of Lord Bergen, sitting with both girls in his lap and Josiah at his feet. He was telling a story, and it was all too much for Elizabeth as the children were hanging on his every word. She was about to object when Aunt Jane came up behind her and said, "Say nothing, the children need this."

What about me? Elizabeth thought, but obediently sat down in the chair opposite and sipped her mulled cider as she watched the dancing flames in the fire. When Lord Bergen finished his story, Elizabeth looked over and the girls were asleep in his lap. She started to stand to pick them up, but he shook his head. Slowly, he stood and began to carry the girls upstairs.

"Let me help you," she whispered.

"No. You relax. Josiah will help me."

Elizabeth was so dumbstruck, she sat straight back down in the chair. He was a natural father, and it was not helping her will to resist him.

When they had left the room, Aunt Jane spoke. "Are you going to tell me what happened out there?"

"I would rather not."

"Humph," she grumbled. "Well, I hope you were as well tumbled as you appear to have been." She giggled.

"Aunt Jane!" Elizabeth reprimanded, but her cheeks burned with embarrassment.

Lord Bergen came back into the room.

They are safely tucked in their beds. I should be on my way."

"No need to rush," Aunt Jane insisted, curse her. She rose to pour him a drink. He would never leave, now!

"Thank you," he said as she handed him a full tumbler of brandy, and he sat back down in the chair opposite Elizabeth.

"I thought I saw Lady Bergen in town today," Aunt Jane said with a recognizable glare. Elizabeth's heart jumped at the thought of a Lady Bergen.

"Aunt Faith? No, you must be mistaken," Bergen replied. "She would never leave London at this season. She hosts the entire family for Christmas."

Elizabeth relaxed.

"Well, I could have been mistaken. I have not seen her in years. We had our come out together, you know."

"No, I was unaware," he answered taking a sip of his drink, then swirling the liquid around in his glass. "I sent her a note telling her I would be detained."

"Then she must have a twin. I could have sworn it was her."

"Dear God, I hope not," Elizabeth heard him murmur. She suppressed a laugh.

Aunt Jane stood up quickly, and Bergen also got to his feet.

"I will be off to bed, then," her aunt said. "My old bones need the rest."

Bergen took Aunt Jane's hand and kissed it. "Good night, my lady."

Aunt Jane gave Elizabeth a knowing wink and then left, shutting the door behind her.

Elizabeth's heart sped up and she could feel the effects of her wassail. Quickly, she pulled the amulet out of her pocket and placed it on the table in front of her.

Bergen was still standing. After a tiny pause, he walked over to her and looked down at her.

"I think you have had enough for one evening, but we are not finished yet."

"Is that a promise?" she asked, instantly wondering where her boldness had come from.

Suddenly, he was on his knees in front of her and his lips were on hers. After she had been thoroughly kissed, he leaned his forehead against hers. "That is most definitely a promise."

CHAPTER 6

eaving Elizabeth and her family, Bergen and Merry headed back to the inn. Bergen had had so much ale of late that he missed the taste of a finer liquor. The brandy had tasted good and he wished he had taken a second glass. His mellowed mood took his thoughts to the kisses he had shared with Elizabeth. He had wished for more time before Marie's interruption but, on the other hand, her appearance had reminded him that there was a need for discretion around the children. He was not used to having children about. Nevertheless, he enjoyed their company, especially Josiah, who seemed to need a male connection. When he had first met Josiah, there had only been one or two-word responses. Now, their discourse covered topics as wide-ranging as horses, travel to London, and the Christmas season. Josiah had mentioned his parents more than once. The pain of his loss was clear. Bergen reminded himself to be especially careful in their relationship so that Josiah was not hurt, again.

As he passed the mulberry bush where he had found Clarence, he checked the area around it. He could not shake the feeling that there was something not quite right with the gypsies who had remained behind. Although he saw no movement and heard no voices, he decided to stop and investigate the space. The discussions about the amulet today had made him uncomfortable for Elizabeth's and her children's safety and the feeling persisted.

A few hundred feet ahead, the road turned, following the edge of a wood, which began to surround the road on both sides. The forested area had occasional dark cavernous openings between trees, only slightly hidden by tall scrub brush. "Wait here, Merry." He dismounted his horse and checked under the brush, gradually walking back behind the thicker undergrowth of the area. A shiny object caught his attention. Kicking away the sandy soil, he discovered a small, bejewelled dagger, one that might have been worn by someone in the troupe. It was not the type of knife that he recognized, but it appeared deadly. *Who would have dropped this?* The hair on the back of his neck prickled, so he mounted Merry and moved her along quickly and quietly. There was an easy access behind some scrub, so he rode Merry into the thicket. They hid behind the thick undergrowth just as two gypsies walked towards them.

"I lost it somewhere out here. I am almost sure." Bergen recognized the voice as belonging to the same man who had spoken outside his window several days past. The two men walked close to the brush, both kicking the soil on the road and studying the edge of the road so intently that they did not notice they had company. It was the first time he had seen the men up close. One was tall and the other was short. They were both dark-headed, and wore thick heavy coats hanging open, revealing baggy shirts and loose trousers. The shorter one, whose voice he recognized, had his head covered by a brown and white turban. The taller one wore a short black cap with flaps covering his ears. *I think I will recognize these two, if I see them again.*

"We need to catch up with the troupe, my brother," the other man grumbled. "We've spent too much time spying on the donkey you abandoned. I'm not sure there was any value to the beast or the *supposed* jewel around his neck. It looked more like a bauble to me, anyway. And you only used the dagger to cut your meat or fruit."

"Then, brother, *you* go back. I will find the amulet. I heard the woman say her son had it. I am certain it has magic powers, and the elders will be glad to have it for our people." The man's tone was terse.

"So be it! Come back to camp tonight and I will spend one more day looking for the stupid amulet, but if you are not successful, we leave. *Agreed?* The man who visits her family each day—I have seen him around. I heard him addressed by the inn's ostler as a lord. We do not need to cause trouble around here."

"True enough." The man whose voice he recognized heaved a sigh. "If the child has it, he may have lost it; but I want to find out. And I want my knife back, even if I only use it for food!"

Bergen needed to warn Elizabeth. What kind of trouble had he brought to her front door with the donkey? Bergen could hardly wait for the two men to walk out of view. As soon as they did, he mounted Merry and rode back to warn Elizabeth.

He looped Merry's reins over the black iron fence and knocked on the door.

The butler opened the door looking a bit startled at his reappearance. "Good evening, sir." He accepted Bergen's hat and coat and stepped back as Lady Newton entered the hall and walked up to the door. "Did you leave something, Lord Bergen," she asked.

He knew she had not meant to ask it quite like that, but he had to admit he liked the Elizabeth with the amulet in her pocket, who could not qualify her remarks to him. He would laugh if this situation were not so serious. He pulled out the dagger.

"I found this on the way home. I thought to look around the mulberry bush area, and while I was looking, the two gypsy men came back. Merry and I hid behind the bushes and overheard them."

"Were they after *that?*" Elizabeth nodded at the knife, a look of alarm on her face.

"Yes, and unfortunately, it is not the real object of their quest. It seems they have been looking for the donkey, but I heard them mention having overheard that Josiah had removed Clarence's amulet. It is my belief they might come for it. I became alarmed and needed to warn you. In fact, I am very reluctant to leave you." Bergen hoped she would see the seriousness of the situation. On the short ride back to Elizabeth's house, he had formed a plan to return there earlier than usual in the morning, knowing that staying, even in the stables, would be out of the question with Elizabeth.

"It is indeed frightening that the men have been close enough to hear our conversations. This afternoon, I heard something stir behind me. It sounded like something stepping across dry brush, but I did not look. Instead, I hurried into the house. Do you think they intend harm?"

"It is unlikely. The travellers are generally peaceful, despite being described as otherwise. They would most likely try to steal the amulet, which from the little I have heard, it seems they feel some entitlement. That does not mean there are no bad people among them, as there are in our own society." Bergen felt a knot rise in his stomach, as he questioned his own decision to return to the inn. "I will keep this..." He held out the dagger. "...with me."

"Thank you for that, sir." Elizabeth smiled gently. "I appreciate you coming to warn us. I believe we will be well. I do have my husband's fowling piece on the top shelf in the boot room. I can secrete it near the door. One of the men will be able to fire it, I am sure. I will also turn Clarence loose in the barn, so he will not be trapped should they try to steal him away. That is all I can think to do. There are quite a few animals—including a baby lamb, a cow, a couple of goats, horses, and a few barn cats that stay in there. Clarence seems to have grown protective and I believe he will warn us of any unwanted guests and protect the other species. Why, only this morning, he chased away a fox."

"Please, Elizabeth, promise me that if they come, you will give it to them."

"I will. I promise." To his utter surprise, she boldly leaned towards him and brushed a kiss across his lips.

"That was nice." Not one to miss an opportunity when it presented itself, Bergen crushed her to him and pressed his lips to hers. He wanted to protect her, and that was a new feeling for him. Out of breath, he pulled back and kissed her nose. "I want you and the children to be safe. Lock the door. I will be back early in the morning."

"I appreciate all you are doing, Lord Bergen..." She sighed.

"Thomas…please call me Thomas," he whispered. Pushing back from the door-case, he took a deep breath. "I'll be back in the morning for rehearsals."

"I will see you tomorrow, then," she murmured.

He watched her close the door and walked around the house to ensure all was secure before he left. There was no sign of the travellers on the way back to the inn, and he had no idea where the band had moved for the night.

"Good evening, my lord." Perry took Merry's reins and patted her mane. "Did you see the fancy carriage over there? Some important guests arrived this morning." The boy pointed to a large black carriage with a gold crest.

"No! Jane was not mistaken; she did see her today," he muttered to himself.

"Begging your pardon, my lord?"

"I was talking to myself, Perry—a bad habit, I fear. Tell me…the lady who arrived today… Did you meet her?"

"I did, my lord. T'was odd-seem'n. She asked if I knew where a *Mrs. Newton* lived, but she looked angry. I was worried for Lady Newton. Tol' her I didn't know the name. She then asked where the church holding a Christmas pageant was, and I pointed out the way to Saint Mary's."

Bergen was impressed by Perry's quick thinking. For some reason he did not want Aunt Faith to present herself at Newton Grange. In truth, he could not imagine why she was here, and why she was angry. Perry did not seem the type to exaggerate, which meant Bergen needed to find out what his aunt was doing here.

The innkeeper and his wife met him at the door, interrupting his reflections.

"My lord, a lady arrived earlier today. She has requested that on your return you join her in the private parlour she has taken for her own use." The innkeeper's wife curtsied.

"Thank you." At least he would have a chance to find out why Aunt Faith was here.

"This way, sir."

He opened the door she directed him to. At his entrance, his aunt put down the wine-glass in her hand.

"Good evening, nephew." She patted the seat next to her. "I need to speak with you."

ELIZABETH SET down the note from Lord Bergen and dropped her head in her hands. After the warnings from him the night before, she had hardly slept for worrying—and now this.

"What is it, my dear?" Aunt Jane asked with concern as she came into the room.

"It seems you were correct. Lady Bergen is in town."

"I knew it! I'm not in my dotage yet!" she cackled.

"Do you see what this means, though?" Elizabeth asked.

"I strongly suspect the old bitty has come to interfere with her nephew's romantic interest."

Elizabeth groaned. "You mean me, do you not?"

"Why else would the old harridan remove herself from her London party, if not to meddle in the heir's affairs?" Aunt Jane rubbed her hands together in anticipation.

"What are you planning, Aunt Jane?" Elizabeth asked warily.

"Why, a little interfering on my own account!" she answered, as though Elizabeth lacked understanding. "What else does the note say?" She came closer and leaned over to look.

Elizabeth held it to her chest. "That he and his aunt would like to pay a call."

"Excellent!" The old lady jumped up as though she were almost young again.

Elizabeth looked on with horror.

"Where are you going?" she asked.

"To get dressed, of course," Aunt Jane said on her way out of the door.

Elizabeth sat down at her dressing table and stared after her aunt, wondering how her life had been turned upside down within a week.

What did all of this mean? Here she was, considering an affair with a London dandy, when, all of a sudden, it seemed everything was out of control. She had nearly allowed him to tumble her against a tree; he had told bedtime stories to the children...and now his aunt had rushed down from London to try to prevent a match? Elizabeth began to laugh hysterically. It sounded like a penny rag!

Elizabeth walked over to the wine cabinet, and pouring herself a small measure of brandy, drank it in one sip. She was going to need fortification to get through this day—she could feel it.

She penned a response to Lord Bergen and after sending it to the Cock Inn, she went upstairs to ready herself for a battle.

After completing her toilette, Elizabeth took one last glance in the mirror as she heard the carriage come up the drive. She did not think she had ever looked so well, even if she was so immodest as to speak thus of herself. Regardless of the outcome with Lord Bergen, she would prove the equal of the finest lady to be found in London. Her gown was of the latest fashion, in a pale blue sprigged muslin, and her hair was pinned up, with a few curls allowed to dangle over her shoulder. The children had been bathed and dressed in their finest clothes, their assistance sought so they would not accidentally spoil the fun. The kitchen had prepared a small feast, and everything was polished to a high shine.

Waiting nervously in the drawing room, Elizabeth was thankful it was not long before Lord Bergen, his aunt and another gentleman were shown in. She did not know what had happened to Aunt Jane, but she could only feel relief and pray she would perhaps escape a dramatic scene after all.

"Lady Bergen, Lord Bergen and Lord Shefford, my lady," the butler announced.

Elizabeth curtsied and the men bowed while Lady Bergen looked down her nose.

"Aunt, Shefford, allow me to present to you Lady Newton," Lord Bergen said in introduction.

"It is a pleasure to meet you," Elizabeth answered. "May I welcome you to Stony Stratford?"

Lady Bergen sniffed.

The aunt was much as Elizabeth had expected. She imagined Lady Catherine de Bourgh, from the novel *Pride and Prejudice*, rushing off to save her nephew from a disastrous mésalliance, and irreverently thought she could well be looking at the character. Lady Bergen was dressed in a manner far too youthful for her age and she wore tight ringlets around her face. The look was not flattering on a young débutante and it was no better on a dowager of advanced years. Elizabeth smiled genuinely and while trying not to laugh caught Bergen's eye. The wicked man winked at her and almost caused her undoing. Giving him a quelling frown and ignoring the flutters of happiness which rushed through her at their shared understanding, she directed everyone to sit down, and sent for a tea tray.

"What brings you to our small town, my lady?" Elizabeth asked innocently, though she knew full well.

"If you must know," Lady Bergen answered sharply, "I wished to discover what was detaining my nephew from his obligations to his family in London."

Shefford cleared his throat, clearly trying to cover a laugh, and Bergen raised his eyebrows at Elizabeth. At that moment, the door burst open and Aunt Jane sauntered into the room as though she were the Queen herself. Her hair had been curled and she wore a gown of teal-coloured silk more fitting for a ballroom. A generous amount of bosom was on display, and peacock feathers adorned a bandeau around her head.

The men rose to their feet and Elizabeth quickly introduced everyone. Aunt Jane stopped in front of Lady Bergen, and bringing her lorgnette to her nose, looked the lady up and down. It was much in the vein of Brummell with his quizzing glass, giving a set-down. Elizabeth exchanged questioning glances with Bergen, her laughter dissolving like ice on the tongue.

"Still trying to display your wares like Haymarket ware, Jane?" Lady Bergen asked coldly.

"At least a trollop gets her man," Aunt Jane retorted.

"Ladies, sheath your claws, if you please," Bergen reprimanded, though he was smiling widely which did odd things to Elizabeth's insides.

Aunt Jane sat down on the settee beside Elizabeth and continued to glare at Lady Bergen.

Fortunately, Henry chose that moment to bring in the tea tray or Elizabeth would have been hard put to cover the awkwardness.

Before any more conversation was begun, the vicar was announced.

"How delightful!" Jane muttered in a sarcastic tone and Elizabeth nudged her to keep quiet.

Elizabeth stood up to greet the man. "Good day, Vicar Brown. To what do we owe the honour?"

"I hope I am not intruding," he said, looking around at their esteemed visitors, who were quickly introduced.

"You are always intruding," Aunt Jane replied.

"There is a seat here, next to me," Lady Bergen quickly offered, no doubt noticing Aunt Jane's treatment of the man. As sure as the day, Aunt Jane sat up straighter and glared.

Instead of trying to make the best of the situation, Elizabeth decided to sit back and watch the entertainment. Lady Bergen began to flirt with the vicar, who lapped up the attention like a wilted flower did water.

Bergen then began to speak to Elizabeth, ignoring the older ladies, who were vying for the vicar's attention.

"I am glad to see all appears well today," he said.

"Yes," she answered. "I warned the servants to keep an eye out for the gypsies. No one has seen or heard anything unusual."

"Very good. I have not seen any more of the troupe since evening yesterday, either."

"Perhaps they will give up and move on," Elizabeth replied. "Why did your aunt come? I thought you sent a note."

"That is why she came. She thinks you are the notorious Mrs. Newton, out to snatch my title and fortune."

"Did you correct her misinformation?" Elizabeth asked, offended.

"She had to come and see you for herself. It seems she was unable to believe I would willingly stay to take part in a Christmas pageant."

"I cannot quite believe it, myself," Shefford put in, scratching his head in comical bemusement. "I must confess, I have never pictured my old friend as a biblical character."

"I am full of hidden talents," Bergen said in his seductive voice while looking straight at Elizabeth. To her annoyance, her cheeks burned in response.

There was another knock at the door.

"Good Lord, who now? I have never seen such chaos in a London house," Lady Bergen snapped.

"Does anyone visit you?" Aunt Jane asked with false sweetness.

Josiah, Marie, and Ruthie were shown in.

"Lady Bergen, may I present my children?" Elizabeth introduced the three and they made their bows and curtsies perfectly.

"You have children?" the lady asked with her hand on her chest.

"They were my late husband's, but I could not love them more were they of my own flesh and blood." Elizabeth smiled at the children.

"How vulgar!" Lady Bergen wrinkled her nose with distaste.

Marie and Ruthie went straight to Lord Bergen as his aunt watched in obvious disgust. She reached into her reticule and pulled out her smelling salts, wafting them beneath her nose.

"Good morning, ladies," Bergen said to Marie and Ruthie. "What have you been doing today?"

"We gathered the eggs and helped milk one of the cowth," Marie answered, precipitating a loud gasp from Lady Bergen. "Then we went to visit Clarence, but he was too buthy to play with uth."

"What was Clarence doing that was so important?" Shefford asked.

"He was trying to cover one of the sheep," Josiah replied.

"Oh! Oh! Get these vulgar creatures out of here!" Lady Bergen demanded, waving her fan as though she would faint. "Bergen, I demand you take me from here at once!"

"As you wish, Aunt. I hope you are satisfied that this lady is not the Mrs. Newton you thought her to be."

"Yes, and I think I prefer the other!"

"The children live on a farm, Lady Bergen. These are natural things for the children to see and know about." Elizabeth tried to defend their prosaic outlook on the countryside.

"Indeed!" Her ladyship looked as though she would soon suffer an apoplectic fit.

With perfect timing, Marie's mouse decided to scurry across the floor and up the lady's skirt. She swooned dead away into the vicar's arms.

CHAPTER 7

*B*efore anyone could react to Lady Bergen's swoon, a flash of white fur flew across the room, under the dress of the lady and then out again, in pursuit of the offending light-grey mouse. Marie shrieked and scrambled after her mouse, while Elizabeth fell over Lady Bergen's protruding feet in a heroic effort to capture Snowball, her cat.

Lady Bergen raised her head briefly, only to swoon once more, to the chagrin of the short round vicar, who was straining to keep her head of tight ringlets from slipping to the floor.

Bergen leapt forward and caught Elizabeth as she fell over his aunt's feet, moments before she hit the floor. Meanwhile, Shefford steadied the vicar and his catch.

"I have her!" Marie held up her mouse, grinning.

"And I have Snowball," Elizabeth whispered. Red-faced, she squeezed her furry white quarry to her chest while Bergen held her close to his.

"Well, it seems you still feel the need to show your wares whenever you have an audience," Aunt Jane quipped at her adversary, holding her arms crossed over her chest. Aunt Faith opened her eyes and raised her head, seeming to forget that she had fainted only moments ago.

"*My wares*? How dare you insinuate such a thing? If you are refer-ring to the ball where you purposely stepped on my dress and stood up, ripping the skirt from the bodice..." She huffed and glared, her face also red, at Aunt Jane.

"Ladies...please." Bergen carefully stood Elizabeth up, squeezing her elbows in a show of affection as he moved towards his aunt. "Aunt Faith, we must leave now to attend rehearsals for the play. Would you care for Shefford and I to accompany you back to the inn?"

Shefford aided the vicar in his attempt to bring Lady Bergen upright. She finally stood, brushing off her skirt with dramatic wipes of her hands.

"I would like to see the play." Without missing a beat, Aunt Faith turned to the vicar, bestowing upon him a slight smile and fluttering her lashes.

"Well, certainly, my lady." The short, round vicar stood straighter, throwing back his shoulders and clearing his throat. "We would love for you to join us. It is the final rehearsal before the presentation to our congregation on Christmas Eve. Guests are always welcome. He held out his arm and she lightly laid her fingers on his sleeve as he walked her to her coach.

Bergen and Shefford mounted their horses and followed behind the coach.

"Bergen, which biblical figure will you represent in the pageant?" Shefford smiled, his eyes full of mirth. "You still have not said."

"No, I have not." Bergen looked at his friend, sure his own eyes must betray the amusement of the situation he found himself in.

"Well..." Shefford laughed. "...are you going to tell me, or are you making me guess?"

"Joseph," he admitted at last.

"I would never have guessed!" Shefford guffawed. "I had you earmarked for a wise man."

"Laugh your fill, my friend. The pageant means a great deal to Elizabeth, and the children—for one reason or another—were not willing to take part. Marie suggested her mother and I do it. That is how this came about.

"I am astonished! I have not seen you take this level of interest in a woman before. I say that with the utmost sincerity, and not in tomfoolery." Shefford nodded and smiled in approval.

Bergen did not want to respond but could not keep from grinning. Thoughts of the kisses he and Elizabeth had shared, and the feelings that her nearness produced, flooded his brain. He was still trying to determine what was happening between them!

They were halfway to the church. Bergen decided to raise the question of the travellers with Shefford and seek his opinion.

"I came upon two gypsies yesterday—one of them was the man who abandoned Clarence in the belief that he was cursed, of all things. He has been watching Elizabeth and her family. I confess I am worried. When I found him, the donkey was wearing an amulet about his neck which may or may not have the power of truth."

Shefford stared at him and then started laughing.

"Wait, Shefford, I am serious. The vicar examined the amulet and found a description in a book which fitted that of the jewel. The amulet seems to elicit truth from the holder, which would appear to be harmless enough. Maybe it is real, maybe it is just the power of suggestion." He told Shefford what he had heard and observed from the travellers since his own arrival.

"The problem is that this same man who abandoned the donkey appears to want the amulet back. I believe he thinks it is valuable and has something to prove, besides." Bergen reached into his pocket and pulled out the jewelled knife. "Then, yesterday, I found a dagger he had dropped on the road near to Elizabeth's house. I find myself worried about her family."

"That is an unusual piece. You are right, this does not sound good. Perhaps the constable should be informed, Bergen. I think you should at least give him the details of what has occurred. If you wish, I could ride to the round-house and fetch him, so you may stay here and protect the lady.

"I agree, he should be brought in. I had intended to see him this morning, but with Aunt Faith's arrival, my plans changed...and now we are almost at the church for rehearsal."

"Yes." Shefford laughed. "Lady Bergen's introduction to Aunt Jane was tremendously entertaining. I would not have missed that, even for a slap-up dinner at Watier's!"

The two men laughed uproariously. "True enough. I had no idea the two knew each other," Bergen said. "The mouse and cat both had better comic timing than any actor I have seen in a long while."

The entourage of eight soon turned into the churchyard, and the two men urged their mounts ahead and secured them in the stable behind the vicarage. The carriage bearing Elizabeth, Aunt Jane and the three children pulled up with Clarence procured behind. Bergen and Shefford assisted the ladies to alight and the small party walked into the church. The vicar met them at the door.

"Are we ready to begin?"

"Yes, Vicar." Bergen took an uneasy look around, hoping they could finish the pageant without any trouble from the two travellers.

The older man extended his arm to Aunt Faith and ushered her into the church and to a front pew.

"Perhaps you will be comfortable here, my lady, while everyone takes up their positions and we can begin."

Josiah appeared. "I put Clarence in the stable until his part, Lizzie. I used the stall next to the vicar's pony."

"Good boy." Bergen was swift to praise, before turning to his aunt. "Aunt Faith, this will take a little while. Are you quite sure you would not rather go back to the inn and rest until we have finished?"

"Away with you!" She playfully swatted her nephew. "I am very interested in the theatrical talents of the vicar and have not seen a Christmas pageant in some time. I have certainly not seen one with real animals."

Beaming, the vicar nodded appreciatively towards Aunt Faith and then offered his arm to Aunt Jane.

"May I seat you, Lady Jane?"

"You certainly may, but I think I would see the play better from that side of the church." Aunt Jane pointed towards a pew.

"Pish. Please do take yourself, and whichever creature is clinging to your head, away from where I am sitting. I have been traumatized enough already this morning," Aunt Faith added peevishly.

Aunt Jane halted, jerking the vicar to an abrupt stop. "On second thought, Vicar, I think I should perhaps volunteer myself to ensure no further drama comes from this quarter to compete with your beautiful play." She turned him back towards the pew Aunt Faith occupied.

"Well, I never!" Lady Bergen blustered.

"Aha! *I knew it!*" Aunt Jane retorted.

"Aunt Faith, Aunt Jane—ladies, please..." Bergen interrupted. "We can all at least be civil for the time we are here." Exasperated, he looked beseechingly towards the two ladies, who now stood facing each other with arms folded against their bodies. "This is important to Lady Newton, the children, and the congregation."

"You are correct, nephew." Recovering, his aunt coyly slipped her hand on the vicar's arm. "Vicar, I believe I would like to sit a little further back. I think it could be cooler nearer the door."

"Yes, please do remove yourself to the back." Then, muttering barely above her breath, Aunt Jane continued, "The air here will be fresher without that dead animal you are wearing."

Bergen suppressed a groan. It must be obvious to all that the entertainment would not be limited to the front of the church.

Shefford tapped him on the shoulder. "I hate to leave, but I will slip out now, visit the magistrate and bring him back with me."

"Thank you. Part of me wishes very much to go with you." He nodded and sighing loudly, moved up the aisle to speak quietly to his aunt. One would describe the inside of the church as small, cosy. Long pews made of dark walnut flanked each side of the centre aisle, with more narrow passages running between the wall and the pews. Tall, colourful stained glass dominated both side walls of the church, each depicting prominent scenes of the Bible on each side, allowing light to filter through. The ceiling was painted with angels and clouds, depicting what Bergen imagined Heaven to look like. Had Bergen not been worried about the possibility of trouble, he might have relaxed and felt more at peace.

ELIZABETH WAS RELIEVED and yet also frightened that the day of the pageant was finally here. She had dreaded it at first and now she did not want it to end. Ending meant that Bergen would be forced to make a decision, and she feared that it would mean he would return home and vanish from their lives.

The members of the congregation were beginning to take their places. The events had moved indoors due to the weather. People came in from the country for such special occasions, and they were beginning to notice their distinguished visitor. Elizabeth saw the looks and whispers as she watched from the side as people were obviously trying to discover whom Lady Bergen was. Lord Shefford had not returned with the magistrate, and Lord Bergen was still hidden until the pageant began. The children were brimming with excitement as they put on their costumes, including false beards which Jane had managed to procure from London. Hannah had sewn the costumes for everyone, including one for Lord Bergen, which no doubt the maid had enjoyed more than she should have. Elizabeth laughed as she tied the rope around her waist to secure the pillow beneath, remembering what had happened the last time, when Lord Bergen had …helped her. Would there be another such opportunity? She should have prepared the children for the fact that he would probably be leaving them soon. Other gentlemen, such as uncles, came briefly into their lives; would they cope as well when he left? Elizabeth knew she would not. Bergen was different—magical—and he made her feel things she had not known existed. She should have guarded her heart.

"It is a little too late for that," she said bitterly to herself.

"Too late for what?" Bergen asked. As he spoke, he put a hand on her back in a shockingly informal way. Her wretched heart betrayed her by beating faster.

"Nothing of any import, sir. I was merely thinking about something I should have brought from home," she prevaricated.

"You look beautiful," he said looking down at her.

"In these rags?" She laughed.

"I think they are fetching," he said as he twirled her around.

Before she thought better of it, she reached up and stroked the beard he had grown over the few days he had been there, in preparation for the pageant.

She jerked her hand back and he caught it. "I should not..."

"Please do not apologize, Lizzie. You may touch me whenever and wherever you like."

She looked away. His flirtations reminded her of why he had stayed. Now she had acknowledged her heart was involved, she must call a halt before it was too late.

"Lord Bergen, I fear there is a matter we need to discuss."

"'Lord Bergen'? That sounds ominous. I feel as though I have been called before my father and am about to receive twenty lashes."

"I doubt this will hurt as much."

He frowned.

"I cannot say how it is you have so easily wormed your way into all of our affections, but I am afraid I must ask you to leave as soon as possible after the pageant."

"I beg your pardon? You wish me to leave?"

"I think it would be for the best."

"Best for whom? Was I so mistaken? Are you playing with *my* affections?"

"How could you ask that? I am not a loose woman to have random affairs whenever it pleases me! I have children to think of!"

He turned and walked to the window. "Even if you think I would toy with you, which might have been a fair assumption before, I would never do that to a child," he defended. "Why do you think my aunt and friend dropped everything and hurried down here? They knew you were different. Something in my notes to them indicated my feelings for you were more than a dalliance. I cannot explain it myself." He turned back to her and spread his hands out. "Have I made a complete fool of myself?"

Tears began to roll down Elizabeth's cheeks and she wiped them away furiously. "It has all happened so fast. I do not understand myself. It does not seem real."

"Do you care for me, Lizzie?" he asked as he drew her close and looked into her eyes.

"Yes, despite myself, I care very much."

He kissed her and then they heard music start in the background.

"We will finish this discussion later. I assure you I am not toying with you. Do you have the amulet?"

Elizabeth nodded and pulled the blue stone from her pocket and handed it to him.

"Ask me anything."

Elizabeth's first thought was mischievous, and she smiled.

"Perhaps that question should wait until later," he said as if reading her thoughts.

"Perhaps," she agreed. "Very well. What are your intentions towards me and the children?"

"I want to be with you and them," he answered without hesitation. Bergen took her hand and tucked the small blue stone in the centre and closed her fingers over it. "I care for you and your family, Lizzie."

The door opened and the vicar yelled, "Take your places, everyone!"

Elizabeth had forgotten about the pageant and the children for a moment. The two girls were standing ready with their shepherd's hooks and their gifts to give the baby Jesus, but she did not see Josiah.

"Where is your brother?" she asked Marie.

"He went to fetch Clarenthe."

"Ah, yes." She relaxed. "Do you remember your lines?"

"We prethent the gifth of gold, myrh, and frankenthenth to our new born king."

"Very good." She bent over and kissed each girl on the cheek as they went to stand in their places. Bergen led Elizabeth outside to the front of the church so they would not be seen until they made their entrance.

"Why isn't Josiah here with Clarence?" Elizabeth asked.

"Perhaps I should go and see. He should be here by now," Bergen agreed with concern.

Elizabeth stood there shivering in the cold despite her layers. She began to imagine any number of horrid things happening with the gypsies, knowing they thought Josiah had the amulet. "That necklace has been nothing but a curse!" she exclaimed angrily.

The vicar opened the front door. "We are ready to begin," he whispered and then looked around. "Where is Lord Bergen? And the donkey?"

"Josiah was supposed to be bringing Clarence to us and he has not come. Lord Bergen went to look for them."

"Oh dear, oh dear," the old man rubbed his hand over his wrinkled brow. "What should we do?"

"There is nothing to do until Lord Bergen returns. Why do you not have the children sing Christmas carols?"

"An excellent idea! Signal when they arrive." He hurried back inside.

"Stop imagining the worst," Elizabeth said to herself as she thought of what the gypsies could have done with her son. He could have been beaten and left for dead, he could have been kidnapped, or worse yet —he could actually be dead.

Elizabeth heard the music begin inside and began to shiver in the freezing cold as snow began to fall. Any other time she would have been excited to see the flakes and a white Christmas. Instead, it only made her fear more for Josiah.

Bergen finally returned, and Elizabeth could tell by the look on his face that something was wrong. "What is it? What has happened?"

"Josiah is missing."

"Oh, no! No, please, no!" she cried into his arms.

"We must be quick in this cold and keep a straight head. You tell everyone inside and organize the men to search. I will go ready the horses." He hurried off with a reassuring kiss on the cheek, and she faced the door.

"Yes, keep a straight head," she commanded herself as she opened it. The crowd turned to face her as she walked into the nave. "Excuse me," Elizabeth shouted over the music and the singing and piano trailed off. "I hate to ruin the pageant, but Josiah has gone missing. Anyone who is able and willing to help search, please meet at the stables as quickly as possible. I fear we have little time in this cold."

This announcement was followed by dull murmurs as the men began to pour outside.

"What has happened, dear?" Aunt Jane asked as her and Lady Bergen rushed to her.

"I wish I knew, Aunt. Bergen thinks it is the gypsies. Can you please take Marie and Ruthie home? I will follow as soon as we find him."

"Of course, my dear."

Elizabeth ran to the stables, and Lord Shefford had arrived with the magistrate. Teams were being organized to search each area, and they were hoping the snow would be useful for tracking Josiah and his kidnappers.

Elizabeth looked around trying to think where her son could be, and she noticed the donkey was also gone. "Bergen, where is Clarence?"

CHAPTER 8

*B*ergen felt sure that Josiah had been taken, and he felt no small measure of guilt for not going after Clarence himself. He should never have allowed the boy to leave the safety of the church. He heard the congregation leave the church and turned to glimpse the activity. Small groups of men hurriedly made preparations—many grabbing canes, large sticks and other impromptu weapons with the clear intention of arming themselves. The grim faces revealed that all were thinking to overtake the kidnappers.

Elizabeth stood near the horses and held her two girls close. She embraced and kissed each girl on the head, and then, taking them by the hand, scurried quickly towards the coach.

"I will help you, Jane." Lady Bergen stood, quickly adjusted her skirts and grabbed her cane from the side of the pew. The two women followed Elizabeth and her two girls to the coach waiting outside.

"Aunt Faith, would you please take Aunt Jane and the girls to the house while we look for Josiah?" Bergen nodded in the direction of his aunt's coach.

"Certainly!" His Aunt Faith reached down and tentatively patted each child on the head.

Bergen nodded again and helped his aunt into her coach. Shefford handed Elizabeth's Aunt Jane into the coach, helped the children up the step and then closed the door. Bergen spoke to the driver. As he did so, within the carriage, he could hear the two ladies talking. Curious, he cautiously peered into the coach window.

"Faith, I would appreciate your help. I am afraid I am not as young as I once was." Jane held out her hand. There was a moment of silence before his aunt responded.

"Thank you." His aunt took Jane's hand. "I suppose we *should* set aside our differences for each other."

"Yes. We should fix our attentions on that sweet little boy." Jane responded.

Aunt Faith sniffed, nodding. She reached into her reticule and pulling out an embroidered handkerchief, dabbed a small tear from the corner of her eye. This done, she reached down and squeezed Jane's hand, again.

Jane opened and closed her mouth, and then nodded. "I will sheath my claws for a while. We should worry about getting the girls home safely and making sure they do not fret over their brother's return."

"My nephew will find him," Faith asserted.

"I hope so," Jane murmured. After a slight pause, she asked, "Do you hear those loud snorts coming from behind the coach?" Without giving Faith a chance to respond, Jane pulled down the window and ignoring the blast of cold air, stuck her head out of the aperture. She soon spotted the source of the commotion. "Look! Clarence is following us. He appears to be intent on something. Strange though it is to say it, that little donkey seems to have taken a liking to our Josiah."

"I am unfamiliar with the area, but is he going in the direction of your house?" Lady Bergen pointed ahead as the little donkey charged in front of her coach.

Jane looked hard at the donkey galloping ahead of them. "Why, yes, he does appear to be going that way." She put her head out of the window again and called to the driver, "Let us go home, James!" She turned to Faith and hid her brimming mirth behind her hand. "I have always wanted to do that." She giggled, drawing an undignified snort from her former nemesis.

"I was so glad to see the magistrate and Shefford arrive. The men must have had an inkling that something was amiss." Lady Faith Bergen clasped her hands together. "I am confident they will find him."

The coach rushed along the road at what Jane considered a headlong pace, its driver clearly trying his best to keep up with the small donkey while at the same time not throwing them all into a ditch, courtesy of the settling snow.

BERGEN WATCHED the cloud of snow rise behind the coach. He wondered what had spurred his aunt to order her coach to fly so fast. Thankfully, her coachman seemed to have it under control. He turned to his lady. *His lady*. That had a pleasurable sound to it.

"How are you feeling, dearest?"

"I confess that I am at sixes and sevens. We must find him." Elizabeth sniffed. "I think some of the travellers have returned. I have seen signs that indicate several people have been camping behind the inn. Let us start there." Bergen checked the security of the saddle, tugging on the straps for tightness, conscious that he would have an additional passenger.

"We cannot waste a moment." Elizabeth wiped away a tear and put her right foot into his interlocked hands. "My poor boy. He could be hurt by those men."

Bergen lifted her onto his horse and swung up behind her, holding her close. Pulling Merry's reins, he leaned forward and smelled Elizabeth's hair. It smelled delightfully of lemon. Suddenly, he realized he wanted to bury his face in her luxuriant tresses. Reprimanding himself, with difficulty, he turned his attention back to the kidnapping.

"Lizzie, Josiah is a quick-thinking lad. I think he will do whatever he can to lead us to where they are keeping him, so keep a watch for any signs, anything odd or peculiar." She nodded and the two of them remained quiet for several minutes. Clearing his throat, Bergen broached another issue which was troubling him. "I realize this is not the best time to mention it, Lizzie, but when we find Josiah and matters have settled again, we must talk further about what has happened between the two of us and, indeed, the question you asked of me earlier."

"Thomas, I am afraid of inflicting further pain upon my children. They have already had too many disappointments in their short lives. I do not mean to disparage your aunt, but as she indicated quite categorically, she was disgusted by my children's parentage. That is exactly what they will face in Society. I have tried to shelter them from the ravages of the *ton* and I will not allow a brief *liaison* with you, no matter how satisfying it might be to me, to cause them further pain or confusion. I have to think of my children." She sniffled quietly into a handkerchief and looked away.

Fifteen minutes or so later, they found themselves on an empty field behind the inn. Trees and the stubble of brush haphazardly filled the area, and tall shrubs surrounded the edges. A cold campfire and a beat-up tin up indicated someone—Bergen supposed it to have been the men from the troupe—had recently camped there but had already left. The state of the campfire site made it appear it had been several days.

"I had hoped to gain information from anyone still camped here." Bergen slid down from Merry and walked about the field but found nothing of significance.

"We should go to the place where I found Clarence. There is an open area behind the mulberry bushes which is hidden from view and that is where I have heard the men's voices. Bergen hoisted himself up and spurred Merry on, passing the Inn and eventually stopping in front of the mulberry bushes. A smouldering camp-fire evinced the gypsies' presence fairly recently. He dismounted and looked about, finding a blue-jewelled, gold earring but nothing else. Bergen pocketed the earring and once more mounted his horse, squeezing Elizabeth closer to him.

"Thomas, I think we should go back towards the house." She pulled the amulet from her pocket and held it up. "This is what they are seeking. They could be thinking that Josiah may have placed it in his bedroom. I thought I saw Clarence racing ahead of your aunt's carriage. He was close to Josiah and appears to have an uncanny omniscience."

"You did not say you saw Clarence." A cold feeling hit the pit of his stomach. "Let us not waste another minute." He squeezed his legs and spurred his horse; moments later, he pulled back on Merry's reins. "That looks like Shefford and the magistrate." Bergen pointed to two riders coming their way.

"Shefford, did you find anything?" he asked when his friend was within hearing distance.

"Nothing that leads us to the boy. We did find gypsies camped on the other side of the river, but there were only women and children. The men were away and had been gone all day. Everyone was keeping mum."

"Lizzie thinks she saw Clarence running towards the house." Bergen shared their own meagre findings. "We were on our way there."

"What are we waiting for?" Shefford urged his mount around and the four riders rode in unison towards the house. Bergen felt guilty for enjoying the ride with Elizabeth, but he did enjoy it.

HELPED from the coach by a footman, the ladies walked swiftly into the house.

"Will my brother be all right, Aunt Jane?" Marie tugged on the older woman's skirt.

"Yes, my dear." Aunt Jane lightly patted the young girls' head. "Your brother will be home soon, I promise. We should stay together. I shall ask Cook to prepare some tea and biscuits."

"Jane..." Faith Bergen waited until Marie took her little sister's hand and walked to the couch. "Jane—wait, do you think your niece or a servant has left the window open?" She pointed to an opened window on the side of the house, with sheer white curtains blowing inwards from the wind.

"Lizzie, open a window in such cold weather? Certainly not! She may love the outdoors, but she has more sense."

"I thought it strange that your butler was not here to welcome us." So saying, Faith put her fore-finger to her lips to indicate quiet, and the two ladies, followed closely by the two little girls, left the room and edged down the hall towards the kitchen area.

Stepping quietly into the kitchen, Faith fetched a frying pan. Brandishing it for Jane to see, she hissed in a whispered voice, "It is a weapon. Are you capable of using it?"

"Of course! You just use your cane and hush!" Jane pointed towards the back of the house. "I heard something hit the floor when we came in. Something is wrong here, Faith. Children, come with me." Leaning down, she hugged the two girls. "I want you to get into the food pantry here, and be very quiet. Do not get up until one of us comes back for you," she whispered as she urged the two girls into the food closet.

Marie kissed Ruthie. "It will be all right, thither," she said, holding her sibling tightly. "Aunt Jane and Lady Bergen will look afther uth." The two girls crouched on the floor of the dark pantry.

"Do not make a sound." Jane gently pulled the door closed.

A crash sounded from the back of the house, where the nursery was located.

"I will lead, and you follow." Jane picked up her frying pan, and Faith duly followed, wielding her cane and holding onto the wall.

"Look!" Jane whispered and pointed.

The door to Josiah's bedroom stood slightly open and they watched a dark-headed man rummaging through the boy's wardrobe. Moonlight from the window made it easy to see him in the dark room. He was wearing a shabby black coat and patched, dark trousers. The man had his back to the women. Faith signalled to Jane and they both charged at the man, Faith relentlessly beating him with her cane, and Jane repeatedly smacking him on the head with the pan. The man screamed and, with his arm protecting his head, tried to escape, but the element of surprise in addition to the weaponry brought him crashing to the floor. Jane kept hitting him until Faith pulled her arm back. "My dear, I think he is quite out of his senses."

"Do you have anything with which we may tie him up?" Faith could not help feeling a sense of accomplishment at what she and her friend had done. Bergen would be surprised.

"Use the curtains," Jane growled. She ripped a blue muslin hanging from the window and tore it into strips. Together they trussed the man up, tightly tying his feet and hands.

"We are a good team, my friend." Faith beamed at Jane.

"You are right, there!" Grinning, Jane nodded and clasped her friend's free hand. "We should probably go back to the girls."

ELIZABETH'S HEART was racing as they rode up the drive through the thickening snow. The entrance door to the house was wide open. Something was wrong.

"Do you wish for me to set you down at the house?" Bergen asked her. "I would prefer you to wait for me, and I see small hoofprints—presumably Clarence's—leading towards the stables, but it looks as if the ladies went into the house by the tracks in the snow and the open door."

"You go on to the stables," Shefford ordered. "We will look in the house."

"Follow Clarence," Elizabeth commanded. She had an odd feeling about the donkey's instincts, and suspected he was following Josiah's scent.

"As you wish, my lady," Bergen said, although he was already heading in that direction.

They dismounted before they reached the stables and Bergen put his finger in front of his mouth to indicate quiet.

"Stand, Merry," he whispered in the horse's ear.

It was eerily silent as they crept forward. With Elizabeth close behind, Bergen walked around the back and after a few yards, pointed a heavy set of footprints in the snow made visible by the soft moonlight.

Elizabeth nodded and had to fight back tears. What had the poor boy been through, and why had the gypsies brought him here?

A muffled groan came from inside the building. Elizabeth then heard a loud smack, as though someone had been hit.

"Quiet, boy! No harm will come to you once we find the stone," a harsh voice barked. "What is taking Piotr so long?"

"He is inside the stable!" Elizabeth whispered.

Bergen nodded and reached inside his coat.

Another muffled attempt to speak was made by Josiah, and this time it sounded like, "Mama." Elizabeth shook with fear. She could not have been more grateful that she had Bergen to help her.

"You go to the front and knock on the door, then run away. I will go in the back and sneak up on him."

When Elizabeth reached the door to the stable, Clarence was already there. On seeing her, he began to jump up and down. There were marks where he had been gnawing at the latch.

"You are a good boy, Clarence. You will have carrots every day of your life!" she praised quietly.

Instead of knocking, she opened the latch and let Clarence inside.

"What in Hades?" the gypsy shouted. Elizabeth thought she caught a thread of fear in his voice as she watched Clarence's little body charge along the gangway at the man.

Bergen had also entered the stable and was creeping towards Josiah, who was gagged and had his hands tied behind his back.

He began to make frantic noises, as Bergen quickly slashed the bonds holding him.

Clarence was holding his own with the kidnapper. "Eeooorrrrrre!" Snorting loudly, the donkey knocked the man off his feet and then, proceeded to kick at him with his hind legs. Falling backwards, the man groaned and rolled over in the straw.

Elizabeth gathered Josiah into her arms and held him close. Josiah whimpered and snuggled into her arms. Bergen took over from the donkey and planted a facer on the villain for good measure. Although Elizabeth thought it unnecessary, she could not blame Bergen for doing so. She would have liked to have done the same. He took a rope from the harness room and tied the man's hands behind his back, then did the same with his feet.

He brushed off his hands then rubbed Clarence on the head. "You are a hero, a little fellow."

"Eeeee!" The donkey squealed and showed his huge teeth in a grin.

"Clarence, guard the man," Bergen ordered.

The donkey nodded and turned to bray at the prisoner.

Elizabeth let out a nervous laugh of relief as Bergen scooped Josiah up out of her arms. He led them back to the house at a brisk march.

"I wonder what Shefford and the magistrate have found."

At that moment, a large group of servants came slowly up the drive, searching with their lanterns as they walked. They had all been given the night off to attend the pageant.

Bergen strode forward to meet one of the grooms. "Take my horse and return to the church and let them know we have found the boy," he said loudly so all could hear.

A loud cheer went up and Elizabeth and Bergen went into the house with Josiah. They heard loud noises upstairs as they moved down the hall and exchanged questioning glances.

"Sit him in front of a fire and wrap him in a blanket," he said quietly. "He is cold and shocked. I will see what else is happening."

"Are you all right, dearest?" Elizabeth asked, cradling Josiah and stroking his hair.

The servants began to pour into the house and dispersed quickly about their duties. Soon, a maid was stoking the fire in the drawing room, another was fetching blankets, and a footman brought Josiah a cup of warm milk.

"I am unharmed. I am sorry I let you down, Mama. Those men came out of nowhere."

"It is not your fault!" Elizabeth exclaimed. "I should have warned you that the gypsies were looking for the amulet. Lord Bergen had suspicions." She wondered if the boy realized he had called her 'mama' for the first time. She was not about to mention it, but her heart filled with love.

"What is so special about that blue stone?" he asked.

"We think it is a truth stone," Elizabeth replied. "They could have had it for the asking!" she said with disgust. "Now they will be transported or hung for kidnapping you." She shook her head. "I was so scared I would lose you!"

"It was not so very dreadful," he said stoutly, trying to comfort her. "I am sorry I ruined the Christmas pageant."

Elizabeth hugged him as hard as she could. "You did not ruin it, dearest, those thieves did!"

"Well, I did say I did not see what all the fuss was about. Maybe I was being taught a lesson."

"Oh, Josiah, that is not God teaching you a lesson! Nevertheless, we can use this to realize how fortunate we are. I would call it a miracle that we found you quickly and you were not hurt."

"Yes, indeed," Bergen said as he came into the room. "I am very glad to see you are unharmed."

"What was all the noise upstairs?" Elizabeth asked.

"Faith and I carried the day!" Aunt Jane exclaimed proudly as she walked into the room, Lady Bergen and Lord Shefford trailing behind. The magistrate was dragging a beaten gypsy down the stairs and out the front door. Aunt Jane moved to the door and held it open. "If you bother our family again, you will have more than a cut lip and crumpled body when they drag you out!" Aunt Jane hollered after the tussled prisoner before closing the door.

"Yes, the ladies are heroines of the finest. They had everything under control when we arrived," Shefford said, smiling.

"Faith is very handy with that cane of hers." Jane smiled at her friend and went on to explain how they had taken Faith's cane and a frying pan and had knocked the man over the head before tying him up. Even more surprising to Elizabeth was the way Jane and Lady Bergen seemed to be cooperating together.

Josiah perked up and shared his story of how he was taken and then how Clarence came in and saved him. He sat up a little taller, a little prouder, and Elizabeth prayed he would not have any lasting effects from the ordeal.

Soon everyone had gathered in the drawing room around the fire, and Henry brought in some wassail and biscuits to cheer everyone up.

"How can we save Christmas?" Josiah asked. "It is ruined. We have not lit the Yule log. I was so looking forward to that part."

"We did gather holly and mistletoe," Elizabeth reminded him.

"I do not see why we cannot light the Yule log now," Bergen said.

"Yes, indeed," Lord Shefford added.

"The servants brought it in earlier," Aunt Jane said.

Marie and Ruth were brought down from the nursery to join in the tradition. The log was lit, and they stood around the fireplace, singing carols. Elizabeth looked at her little family, their faces glowing from the warmth of the flames, and began to think it was the most special Christmas she could remember. She was nervous for what might lie ahead with Thomas, but she had borne the burden alone for the past year and it felt good to lean on someone else. Her gaze rested on Josiah and she had to swallow a lump in her throat. It was hard to contemplate what might have happened if Bergen and Lord Shefford had not been there.

Rising from her chair, she said to the children, "It is growing late, it is time for bed." All three protested, predictably, but obeyed and made their way to the nursery in front of her. "Tomorrow, we will go to church and deliver the baskets to the poor," she told them.

"And see the pantomime on Boxing Day," a sleepy Marie added.

Once the children were safely tucked into bed, Elizabeth returned downstairs to wish everyone good night, only to find that Lord Shefford had escorted Lady Bergen back to the inn, and everyone else had discreetly gone to bed.

"Very handsome of them to have left us alone," Bergen remarked.

Following his gaze, Elizabeth saw some mistletoe hanging above them. A moment later, he placed a gentle kiss on her lips.

She laughed. "I think everyone is exhausted from the excitement."

"Forgive me," he said, pulling her into his arms. "I was being selfish."

"I do not mind," she said softly. "In fact, I do not want you to leave."

CHAPTER 9

"*A*re you sure?" His body suddenly thrummed as he brought her closer to his lips, at the same time combing back the hair from her face with his fingers.

"Yes, sir. I am quite sure. The children are abed, Aunt Jane will be asleep by now, and I…" She hesitated. "Call me a hussy if you will, yet I cannot bring myself to send you away." She turned her face up; her eyes were closed and a contented smile curved her lightly closed lips.

Bergen wanted her. Leaning over, he kissed her, slowly at first, sweetly touching and tasting. Covering her lips fully, he possessed her soft mouth ever more ardently. She yielded to the pressure of his lips, allowing his tongue entry. Their tongues met, caressed, parried and teased, wantonly exploring the recesses of each other's warm mouth. Reaching down with his right hand, he slowly raised her dress, gliding his hand up the inside of her leg, and with practised caresses, working his way to her hidden treasure. He was certain he would find it moist and accommodating.

Elizabeth gave a slight gasp, but held tightly on to his arms, keeping him from stopping, and not letting his lips leave hers.

Bergen felt his heart beating harder; he could even hear it. Elizabeth broke off the kiss and turned away, her breathing rapid and heavy.

"We cannot stay in the drawing room. A child could wake up."

"You are right, of course." While he was panting from anticipation and his heart was threatening to leave his chest, Bergen realized this was more than mere lust. He cared—for and about Elizabeth, and the children...a great deal.

"We cannot stay downstairs. We should retire upstairs." Elizabeth dropped her hands to her sides and with a shy smile, leaned towards him, placing her head on his chest. "Please, Thomas. I do not want you to leave... I hope you are not shocked. I promise you, I am no wanton. You make me feel—" She broke off and turned her face into his chest. He felt her warm breath through his shirt and almost lost control.

"I do not want to leave. I am honoured, not shocked, and I should like nothing more than to stay, but I think we should talk about it first. There will be no turning back for me, if I take you upstairs."

"I will have no regrets, my dear sir," she murmured.

"What about the children?" His voice cracked. "You are right. They deserve far better than an occasional 'uncle'." She looked into his eyes but said nothing. It turned his insides to mush. Dropping to one knee, he cradled both her hands and smiled up at her. "Lady Newton, I have never met a woman like you—one so generous of spirit and of heart. You are clever and beautiful, and I have no doubts you will make any man a fine wife...but I want you for my own..." He paused; he had not given thought to marrying anyone before this moment. Yet the events of this day had revealed what was in his heart about this woman and her family. Even her aunt had won him over. What had started as a desire for a Christmas tryst had changed into so much more. He wanted her. *I love her*, he realized with sudden, stark clarity. "Lizzie, please make me the happiest of men by agreeing to be my Countess."

"Thomas, you do not have to offer marriage," Elizabeth returned. Large tears ran down her cheeks as she spoke.

He dabbed away the wetness and pulled her hands to his lips, placing kisses on the back of each.

"I want you, Lizzie, yes. I hunger to take you for my own, but I realize that I want more than just your body to warm my blood. I want you to be part of my life for always."

"You want me forever?" She smiled through a new veil of tears. "No one has ever wanted me for my own sake."

"Then your husband was a fool! He neglected a remarkable woman. You are wonderful, Lizzie. Your children are wonderful." He grinned. "I want to be the one who teaches Josiah to fish and handle a horse. I want to help keep the girls feeling safe and loved for who they are, and I want you, Lizzie Newton, to be my life's partner."

"Yes."

"I do not want to start our life together by repeating their father's actions, and in their home." He stopped. "Wait! You said, 'Yes'?"

He stood up, his gaze on her beautiful face, hardly able to breathe. "Yes?"

She nodded. "Yes! A thousand times, yes," she whispered against his lips.

"My dearest, I will do my best to make sure you will never be sorry." He pulled her close and covered her lips with his own.

The sound of footsteps in the hall startled them and they quickly separated. A moment later, dressed in her nightgown with a robe around her, Aunt Jane stuck her head inside the room.

She winked at her niece. "Keeping him for yourself, are you, dearie?" She chortled and nodded, clearly pleased with her discovery.

"A...Aunt Jane, you are mistaken..." Elizabeth stuttered, immediately looking away.

"I think not, my child. Your red face tells me all I need to know!" She gave an excited chuckle.

"Aunt Jane, if I may save my lady's blushes...?" Bergen spoke up. "Lizzie has agreed to be my wife. I have asked her to marry me."

Without hesitation, Aunt Jane set down her candle and embraced her niece, hugging her tightly.

"Gel, you have certainly picked a handsome one." She turned to Bergen. "This gel has the heart of an angel. I am happy for both of you. When is the happy event?" She looked at each of them.

They exchanged glances. Elizabeth's mouth fell open in mock dismay.

"Ah…we have not discussed a date, Aunt," she said at length. "If it suits everyone, however, I should love to be married before the festivities end. Christmas has become my favourite time of year."

"Twelfth Night would be perfect! What a lovely idea to end this Christmas with your nuptials!" Aunt Jane slapped her hip, and smiled, clearly pleased. "This will be such wonderful news for the children. They have grown attached to this one." She nodded wryly in Bergen's direction. "I was considering him for myself, if the truth be known." At this, she cackled loudly in evident delight. "Very well, my dears, I shall say goodnight."

Bergen waited until Jane's footsteps had receded up the stairs. "I can foresee she will be a corky one to have hereabouts." He grinned.

"She can be difficult, but life is never boring with her in the house." Elizabeth lifted her arms around his neck. "Kiss me once more before you leave."

"Gladly." The smell of outdoors and lemon flooded his senses, and he felt his body quickly respond. He leaned down and met her lips in a kiss designed to leave her wanting more. To his intense satisfaction, she released her breath in a manner suggesting both contentment and longing.

"I will return tomorrow. I hope the children will be as accepting as Aunt Jane." Hugging her tightly, he kissed her head in a gentle affection belied by his previous passion.

"You have already won their hearts," she responded. "They will be in high ropes. You had better leave before I decide not to let you go."

"You can have no idea how tempted I am to stay, my dearest, but I wish our marriage to begin in the right way—for us as well as for the children."

"You spoke of my heart, but I do not know of any other gentleman who would accept another man's illegitimate children and bring them up as his own."

"Well, I know a lady who has been doing so, and I happen to love her."

"You do?" Elizabeth blinked away a tear. "I love you, too."

His heart warmed. Never had he considered hearing those words would matter to him, but since meeting Elizabeth, the thought of marriage had kept slipping into his mind. In the beginning, he had easily managed to push such notions aside. Now, however, he could not imagine even wishing to do that.

"I will leave early tomorrow and procure a special license. I expect Shefford will probably go with me because he will not credit it." He laughed. "I wonder how surprised he will be at our news."

The road back to the inn that night was bright under the pearly light of the moon. It gave Bergen time to think. His heart was so full of happiness. The day had been long, but to his thinking, it had been one of the best days of his life. He passed the mulberry bush where he had found Clarence and smiled. If not for that little donkey, none of this would have been possible. There were no voices coming from behind the bush tonight. Bergen heard only the song in his heart.

ELIZABETH AWOKE feeling she wanted to pinch herself. She threw back the covers and ran to the window with all of the giddiness of a child on Christmas morning. The ground was covered with white snow crystals, a perfect blanket as far as the eye could see. It was almost as if the scare of the day before had not happened. Last night had, however. She had not imagined Thomas down on one knee, asking her to become his wife, although such an occurrence was the stuff of dreams. With finger and thumb, she nipped her forearm. No, she was not dreaming. Long ago she had given up on finding love; it had seemed as if it was only something to read of in novels.

Snuggling her wrapper around her and smelling the sweet, spicy aromas of festive baking which were drifting up from the kitchen, she smiled.

"Please let it be real," she whispered. The pitter-patter of little feet in the nursery above indicated the children were also awake and excited. Christmas Eve had not been typical, and she would try to make amends today.

As Elizabeth was dressing for church, Marie came bursting into her room. "Mama! The wathailers are here! Hurry, come quickly!"

Elizabeth smiled at the child's exuberance and followed along. She had no doubt that the wassailers would not leave before they had received the handsome vails they were accustomed to from Newton Grange.

In the wide sweep of the drive before the house, a group of merry villagers were singing, 'Oh, come all ye faithful.' The servants were handing out warm wassail and biscuits. Elizabeth was glad they had improvised and come this morning instead.

"Look, Mama!" Josiah exclaimed. "There is Lord Bergen and Lord Shefford, carrying a tree! Why would they do such a thing? We already have a Yule log."

"I cannot imagine what he is about," Elizabeth replied. "I will let him explain."

"Why do you have a tree, thir?" Marie asked with an adorable furrow in her brow.

The wassailers parted to let Shefford and Bergen pass, and they shook the snow from the tree before walking into the house. The children watched, their eyes wide and full of curiosity.

"This," Bergen said as they set the large tree down with gasps of relief, "is a Christmas tree."

"Why do we need a tree in the house for Christmas?" Marie asked.

"My grandmother was German, and this is one of their traditions. They bring a tree in and decorate it and put presents underneath it."

"Oh, I think I like that tradition," she said in a decided fashion.

Bergen smiled at her and then nodded to some servants who entered the room holding ribbons, candles and fruit.

"You hang these things on the tree." He nailed the tree to a makeshift stand, then took some decorations and demonstrated to the children.

"It ith beautiful!"

Elizabeth observed the scene and tried not to cry. This thoughtful man had given her family a Christmas these little ones would never forget.

Shefford and Bergen were placing the decorations at the top of the tree, while the children filled the bottom branches. Elizabeth liked this tradition very much. The gentlemen were even singing with them. Then she heard a banging on the window pane, and there was Clarence, trying to join in the fun. She lifted the sash and he poked his nose inside so she could pet him. He seemed to dance along when the children attempted to sing, 'Joy to the World.'

Elizabeth's heart was so full, she was sure it was bound to burst. The older ladies soon joined them, seeming to have made some sort of truce over their shared experience capturing one of the thieves the night before. Time would tell how long that would last.

"Are we ready to break our fast?" Elizabeth suggested at length, in a vain attempt to gather the children. "Cook has prepared your favourites this morning!"

"Wait a moment, please. Peters," Bergen called to his man. "Have a seat, all of you, if you will. I have something for each of you." He took a bag from his man and handed a package to each child.

"Gifts on Christmas Day? Is this another German tradition?" Elizabeth asked, wondering when the man had had time to arrange all of this.

"Just a token to show my appreciation, and yes, in a manner of speaking."

Josiah pulled out a beautiful, hand-carved bow and arrow set, and looked as if he would cry.

"Thank you, sir."

"I thought you might enjoy hunting. You can help earn your keep," Bergen told him with a teasing wink.

"Ruth and Marie, these are for you." They both opened their presents, which were beautiful dolls that looked like the girls themselves. They instantly hugged them to their bodies and smiled at Bergen.

"Thank you, thank you, thir."

"Aunt Jane, this is for you."

She opened a box and withdrew a bright blue scarf. "My favourite colour! Thank you."

"Last, but not least, this is for you." He held out a small fabric pouch, tied with a ribbon, to Elizabeth.

She opened up the pouch to find a beautiful ruby and diamond ring.

"It is the Bergen betrothal ring. Fortunately, Aunt Faith happened to have it with her. Children, your mama and I are going to be married—if I win your approval," he said with a wry smile.

"Oh, yeth!" Marie exclaimed.

Ruthie nodded her head around her thumb, which was deep in her mouth.

To Elizabeth's astonishment, Josiah jumped up and gave Bergen a hug.

It was hard to think about the real meaning of Christmas after such a morning, but the vicar gave an excellent sermon—despite Aunt Jane's accusations—and they went home to partake of a feast of turkey, duck, plum pudding, marchpane, and gingerbread.

CHAPTER 10

*B*ergen felt in his pocket and his fingers curled around a folded paper. *The special license.* It had not been as quick as he had thought it would be to secure it, only because the bishop had been visiting two local parishes to perform seasonal services. It had delighted Bishop Stephens to hear of Bergen's upcoming nuptials. The visit had been happy, but poignant at the same time, for he learned something he had not previously known. Bishop Stephens had been the parish priest who had married Thomas' own parents. The bishop's comportment throughout his visit, therefore, was not unlike an extension of Bergen's own family, as the clergyman wanted to know all about the woman Bergen planned to marry as well as the latter's motive for the marriage. Nothing seemed prohibited to Bishop Stephens. Recognizing the clergyman's sincerity, his concern had moved Bergen. To find that it was to be a love match settled the matter for the bishop, and he happily handed the special license to Bergen.

Hearing stories of his parents only reminded him how much he still missed their laughter and the wonderful joy experienced in heart and soul when he had been in their presence. His heart faltered on the memory. Realizing he needed to shake off this melancholy, he looked over at Shefford, who had gone with him, and now seemed to be almost nodding to sleep.

"Shefford!" he said sharply. "Must I prod you to wake you, friend?"

"Wake me? I have been waiting for you to travel back to me, Bergen. You have worn the same distant look ever since we left Bishop Stephens. Are you having doubts, *mon ami?*"

"No. Remarkably, I am very excited—something I never thought I would be over becoming leg-shackled. I apologize for my distance. He spoke of my parents. With their deaths being so sudden and recent, I am afraid it got the better of me. I fear I must have the sensibilities of an old woman." As his friend chuckled, Bergen reached into an inner pocket, extracted the license, and waved it at Shefford. "Let us indeed be merry!" He carefully replaced the document and felt his mood elevate at the same time. "Thank you for going to London with me, Colin. You are a good friend and I appreciate your company more than words can say."

Shefford moved his horse closer. "Bergen, you have always been like a brother to me. I can say now, that when your aunt contacted me and told me of her plans to flush out this wanton widow from your life, I knew you would need reinforcements. I also wanted to make sure you were well," he admitted sheepishly. "I like Lizzie and her children, but I am most amused by Clarence. The donkey seems almost human."

"Yes, he has reminded me of that fairy tale about the frog prince— you know, the prince who irritated a witch and she turned him into a frog. Then, to find that he carries with him a rock that makes you tell the truth—it only added to the amusement."

They both laughed uproariously.

"The truth is always better. Perhaps we should pass it to your Aunt Faith and find out what the real story is between her and Lizzie's aunt." Shefford's eyes sparkled with mischief.

"Now, that would be amusing!" Bergen nodded thoughtfully. "I may just do that!" He nudged Merry and they covered the remaining distance from London with greater celerity. The wedding would be this afternoon and he had much to do.

"We are almost there. Clear skies, brisk weather, and license in hand...I could be wrong but this trip was quicker than yesterday's—only a few hours. Do you mind if we stop at the inn and call on Aunt Faith? We could also do with a bite to eat. I am not due at the church until almost noon. I do not want to arrive too early and throw Elizabeth's household into an uproar. She has enough to deal with already, organizing the children and Aunt Jane." Bergen sniggered.

"Yes... I am wondering if that woman has set her cap for the vicar." Shefford looked over at him, a serious air about him. "I am all for people finding happiness and I have not missed the glances he gives her."

"I believe you are right, but I do not plan to interfere. Aunt Faith was also showing some interest, although I am strongly of the suspicion she is doing it to irritate her friend. Therein is another reason I would love to tease out the history between the two." Bergen smirked. He loved his aunt, but her meddling had always nettled him and the thought of turning the tables in fun was irresistible. She was his favourite relative, and he was sure she would see the sport in his game.

Fifteen minutes later, they arrived at the inn and dismounted, handing the reins of their mounts to Perry.

"My lord, welcome back. Your aunt has the inn hopping this morn." He smiled and then bit his lip. "I apologize, my lord. I forgot my place and misspoke."

Bergen grinned. "It is already forgotten, Perry. My aunt has a forcible effect on people, especially when she is on a crusade." He reached into his pocket and handed a shilling to the young ostler. "Thank you for your good care of Merry. Our horses have been to London and back these past two days. Please give them a thorough rub down and a mash."

"Thank you, my lord. I will see to them, all right and tight." Perry gave him an impish smile. "I hear congratulations are in order."

"Yes, thank you." It would be the best of days. *I am getting the woman of my dreams*, he thought, overcome with happiness.

The two men made their way into the inn. Alice, his aunt's maid, met them at the door.

"Oh! My lords!" She made a quick curtsey. "Your aunt, my lord, is waiting for you in the parlour. She pointed to the private parlour behind her. At the same moment, there was the sound of breaking glass.

"Damn it! Now it is all over my dress. Bumbling idiot!" They walked into the room to find Aunt Faith fuming over a pool of spilled tea. The parlour was otherwise empty.

"Aunt?" Bergen stepped up behind her and gave her a warm kiss on the cheek. "May we help?"

"Oh! I apologize, my dears. I am afraid my good manners have exited this morning and my clumsiness has taken over." His aunt looked up at him tearfully.

"Aunt Faith! What has you so out of sorts?" Bergen was immediately concerned.

"I am so sorry. It is mere foolishness. I was thinking of your dear mother and father and how happy they would be to for you today. Then I became maudlin and dropped my cup of tea. I have ruined my dress and there is not enough time to clean it. It was my season favourite." He had never seen his aunt so upset.

"Aunt Faith, my parents have been on my mind also," he said, holding her tightly, "I believe they are with us still." He held her out from him and tried to look stern. "You know what Father would say if he heard you cursing." Bergen tried not to laugh. He knew his aunt employed the language of the stables on occasion when she was upset, and had done so for as long as he could remember.

"I want the day to be perfect...and then there is Jane. I cannot let her look...better than I. There, I said it; but I will never admit to such a thing, even with witnesses." She winked through her tears at Shefford.

Bergen felt a heel for even considering tricking this wonderful lady with that truth stone. "Aunt Faith, I know the ways of you ladies well enough to know you will have brought trunks full of dresses. I am sure you will have one which will take the place of this one." He smiled impudently at his aunt.

"Silly boy, of course I have. You must know pink is my best colour, even in my dotage, and I did wish to look...my best."

"Dotage? Pshaw!" Bergen turned to his aunt's maid. "Alice, please see if the innkeeper's wife can join us. And ask for some scones and more tea—and some ale for Lord Shefford and myself." He paused. "We have not yet eaten this morning."

"Yes, my lord." She curtseyed and hurried off to do his bidding.

Alice returned with the innkeeper's wife, both bearing platters of hot food, including scones for his aunt.

"Mrs. White, if I may..." He delayed the innkeeper's wife as she was leaving. "Would you know of anyone in town who can remove tea from satin?"

Turning to his aunt, she appraised the dress, still dripping with hot tea. "My lady, if you will permit me, I believe I can clean that for you. I used to be a seamstress in my youth, and if I say so m'self, I was good with stains."

"Oh, yes, indeed. That is very kind. I shall send the dress to you immediately." His aunt turned to leave with her maid but paused when halfway to the door. Reaching into her pocket, she withdrew a small black bag. "For you, Thomas. These were your mother's, and before that, my mother's. I wore them at my wedding, and your mother did before that, and your grandmother before that. I had hoped to give them to your bride, but maybe they would be better coming from you."

Tears threatened, and he swallowed and waited a moment before speaking. His heart was suddenly full. "Aunt Faith, would you give them to Lizzie? I think she would like that very much."

"Truly? It would be an honour. Thank you, nephew." She bobbed her head in appreciation, seemingly unable to speak.

Bergen watched his aunt and her maid leave the room and he felt a renewed wave of good fortune and happiness wash over him. He still had his family. His parents were with him in his heart, and his aunt was here. Silently, he vowed he would make sure that from now on she would be far more a part of his life. He looked at his friend.

"Shall we?" Without hesitation, as though literally starving, the two men attacked the meats and cheeses in front of them. They had been up since before dawn and noon was still two hours away.

ELIZABETH HAD HAD a fashionable wedding full of pomp and circumstance the first time. This time, her perspective was different. This marriage was because she wanted it and cared for the man fate had thrown in her path. She hoped, *this time*, to keep him for life. Now she understood better the feelings Horace had entertained for his mistress. Had Horace been able, he would have married her; Elizabeth had been the bride made for connections, not caring.

This ceremony would be simpler, a reflection of the affection between Elizabeth and Thomas. Surrounded by friends and their family, it would have more meaning. Elizabeth smiled. Not only had she been given a second chance at marriage, but Thomas also accepted her unique menagerie was a part of her.

Hannah helped her to dress in a simple cream silk gown, adorned with a lace overdress studded with tiny pearls. They went beautifully with the necklace Lady Bergen had given her. Elizabeth had been very touched by the kind words and welcome she was receiving into Thomas' family, especially after the way his aunt had come here to prevent such an alliance. Elizabeth laughed aloud and shook her head.

"What is so funny, my lady?" Hannah asked.

"I was thinking of the rivalry between Aunt Jane and Lady Bergen when she first arrived."

"They seem to be rubbing along better, now," Hannah observed as she put the final touches on Elizabeth's coiffure.

"Indeed, they are. I cannot help but wonder about Aunt Jane. She wants to stay here instead of removing to Rose Ridge after the wedding."

"Can you not hazard a guess, my lady?" Hannah asked slyly. "Her and the vicar…" her voice trailed off.

"Truly?" Elizabeth asked in surprise.

"Oh, yes! That badgering is all for show."

Elizabeth was certain her mouth was gaping.

"Mayhap they will wed once you are all settled. I think she felt it her duty to look after you.

"I wish I had known!"

"Well all's well that ends well, as they say. Now you had best be getting along or you will be late for your own wedding."

Elizabeth's eyes filled with tears despite herself and she reached over and gave her maid a swift hug.

"You look even more beautiful than you did at your first wedding. Now, away with you!" With the license granted a trusted retainer, Hannah shooed her out of the room.

The children were waiting to ride with her to the church and were dressed in their new clothes, which had been made especially for this occasion. Elizabeth was wrapped in fur and her hands were kept warm by a matching muff. Outside, a sleigh stood ready for them and Clarence was nearby with a large bow around his neck. Elizabeth did not even comment. It was only fitting that the little creature who had brought them together be present.

"When did we acquire a sleigh?" she asked.

"Lord Bergen had the smith attach the runners to an old carriage," Josiah answered. "It was a surprise."

"It is perfect." He seemed to have thought of everything. A small sliver of doubt crept in as she reflected that she had only known this man a fortnight, and she was about to give herself to him for life. Not only herself, she thought, but her children too. She had not even seen their new home, but she had little doubt it would be finer than anything she had known. She hoped she would be able to maintain a semblance of simplicity, because she had found peace in it. There again, she had never really known Horace at all, even after marriage.

They soon arrived at the church, and Elizabeth was shocked to see her brother waiting there to hand her down. She had sent a note, of course, but had not expected any of her family to come. Her parents were elderly, and the roads were still covered in snow in many parts. They had sent a return note with their regrets and best wishes. Hannah escorted the children inside.

"Richard! I cannot believe you were able to come!"

"I would do anything for you, Lizzie. Besides, Bergen is an old friend. We belong to the same club."

"Of course you do," she muttered sardonically to herself. She began to walk into the church, but Richard stopped her.

"Lizzie, can you tell me you are truly happy? I know your first marriage was not ideal." He looked at her with concern.

"Oh yes, brother, I am deliriously happy. It is very different this time."

He looked at her hard and seemingly satisfied, kissed her on the forehead. "Shall we?"

Taking a deep breath, Elizabeth replied without hesitation. "Yes. I am ready."

The doors to the church opened, and her eyes adjusted to the light as they walked in. The small nave was full to bursting with people, many of whom she did not recognize.

"I was not expecting…"

"Such a crowd?" he asked. "A great part of London Society has come to see who has captured one of the most elusive bachelor earls. Bergen is well-liked, you know."

"I-I suppose I should not be surprised."

"Do not think about them, dearest sister. Keep your attention on Bergen."

Elizabeth smiled. That would be easy to do. She looked up to see his handsome face as the music started and they proceeded down the aisle. He was wearing simple attire by London standards, but he stood out nonetheless. Shades of silver, grey and white had never looked so appealing, she thought.

As she reached the altar, she heard Marie's voice and turned to smile at the children who seemed to be as happy about the marriage as she was. As she faced Thomas, her brother passed her hand to him. She felt something smooth yet hard as they joined hands, and she looked down to see the blue amulet shining up at her.

"So, there is no doubt in your mind," he whispered in her ear.

She soon forgot about the large congregation as they stood close together. His comforting warmth reassured her and spoke of things to come. Elizabeth knew she was gazing longingly at him and allowing her feelings to show, but she could not help it.

As they made their vows to love and cherish each other, Elizabeth knew they both meant them. How different this marriage would be!

When they were pronounced man and wife, the congregation began to sing. Almost instantly, Elizabeth heard a tapping on one of the windows. She was not the only one who heard; her new husband raised his eyebrows in a comical expression. Turning together to look for the source of the offending noise, Elizabeth and Thomas saw Clarence's nose and teeth pressed up against a glass pane. Before Elizabeth could tell him not to, Josiah ran to open the window and the little creature at once pushed his muzzle over the sill into the church. Elizabeth looked at Thomas and they laughed.

"It is only fitting," he said, his voice laced with amusement.

"Indeed, it is," Elizabeth agreed, chuckling.

Clarence lifted his head and began to bray. The sound clearly resembled 'Joy to the World,' and it was so loud, the congregation stopped singing to look around in wonder. The villagers laughed and pointed, while some of the Londoners were horrified. The children did their best to quiet him, but Clarence continued to bellow the song he had heard the children sing some days before. When he had finished, Thomas explained to the congregation.

"This little donkey brought Elizabeth and I together. He is very welcome at our ceremony, and at our home forever."

The congregation broke out in cheers and laughter. Amidst the tumult, Thomas swept her down the aisle and out of the door. Those towards the rear of the church followed, offering congratulations and tossing rice at them as they clambered into the sleigh.

On their return, they found a breakfast feast had been prepared, and they were joined by many of the Londoners Elizabeth had never met.

A long line of handsome, charming, and roguish earls paraded before her and later proceeded to dance with her, regaling her ears with stories of Thomas' exploits.

"May I cut in?" Thomas asked as she danced with one of his best friends, the Earl of Weston, who himself had only recently married.

"I have not finished," Weston said and turned her away from Thomas.

"Would you care to meet me at dawn?" Thomas teased.

"I have not completed my story," Weston parried.

"Precisely. Now, go away. I cannot wait to put my hands on my wife."

"Thomas!" Elizabeth chastised, her cheeks flaming.

"Speaking of which, *my* wife looks as though she needs some touching," Weston said as he relinquished his prize and strode away.

"You two are horrible," she said, rapping him on his arm with her fan.

"Yes, but horrible in a good way. I cannot wait to show you," he whispered, and grinning wickedly, kissed her in the middle of the drawing room, in front of God and half of fashionable Society.

Instead of being appalled, raucous cheers and shouts of encouragement came from his group of fellow earls.

Several minutes later, Elizabeth looked around the room for the children.

"Aunt Jane and Aunt Faith took them away some time ago so we can be alone for a while," Thomas said, easing her fears. "Everyone here is a close friend and will not judge you. I would not have done it were they likely to."

Elizabeth glanced about her, and it appeared he was correct. No one was looking at them with anything but happiness, if they were even looking at all.

Weston was now standing by the fireplace, openly adoring his own wife, and Shefford was flirting with a London beauty.

"I think it is time we take our leave. I am ready to start the next chapter."

Elizabeth gave him a quizzical glance.

"The one where I have you and hold you and cherish you all the days of my life."

Elizabeth was not about to argue with that. She took his proffered hand and they quietly left the room. If anyone noticed, they were tactful enough not to draw attention to the fact, and the two of them walked up the stairs without hindrance. Reaching her bedroom, Thomas closed the door, locking out the rest of the world.

"Help me with this, husband," she said softly. Turning her back to him, she leaned her head forward.

"I would love to." Bergen kissed her neck as he loosened her laces, divesting her of the gown, and then her corset. The touch of his hands sent delicious tremors along her arms to her neck, and onward down her back, crowning in her nether regions. Trembling with happiness and desire, she pulled her petticoats and shift over her head, leaving her with only her stockings. Reaching down, she began to roll them off.

"Wait. Please, leave the stockings. Allow me to take them off...but later."

Her husband removed his boots and stepped back, loosening his neckcloth. He pulled it off and tossed it over his shoulder, seeming not to care where it landed. Lifting his shirt, he pulled it over his head and threw that in the same direction as his neckcloth.

"Can I ask you something?" Elizabeth hesitated, yet the pin he wore had puzzled her since she had first seen it nestled in the folds of his cravat. "What is the significance of the pin?"

"It is my club pin. But it no longer signifies, since to wear it, one has to be single." He took it off and tossed it on the side table. "Now. Where were we?" With his free hand, Bergen reached down and opened the flap of his breeches.

Elizabeth grabbed his hand. "It is my turn, if you please, husband," she said, barely lifting her lips from his. Reaching out, she tugged down his breeches. Gently touching, she then freed his manhood, before slowly pushing his trousers to the floor.

"Be careful, my love, or we might be done before we even start." Bergen winked at her, and pulled her backwards onto the bed with him, rolling over her. For a second or two, he hovered over her waiting lips before covering them with his own, gently kissing and nibbling until she allowed his tongue entry to her warm mouth. His tongue swept the cavity of her mouth, and she eagerly joined him, both tongues intimately tantalising and touching as with one mind they stirred warmth and teased each other to a heated passion.

By the time their kiss ended, they were both heaving with pent-up desire. Bergen leaned back a little and with half-closed eyes, ran a finger up her body, from her legs to her neck and back again. *I have never known such pleasure, and this is only the beginning,* she thought, gasping as Bergen's hand stopped to fondle her breasts on the return journey. Circling and teasing the nipple with his fingers, he then leaned down and took it in his warm mouth, suckling and lightly nipping before moving to the other one. Elizabeth could not help herself. Her thoughts reverted to Horace and she was sure he had never touched her in such a fashion. His movements had been abrupt and self-centred. Bergen was making love to her. *Her!* The normal chill in this room was gone...only heat remaining—lots of heat, surrounding her.

Elizabeth felt well and truly loved—the two of them stoking each other's passion, kissing, playing, and loving in ways she had never even imagined. All night they continued their lovemaking, until finally they lay spent, smiling and exuding happiness in the afterglow of their sated hunger.

At length, Elizabeth rolled over and kissed her husband. "I love you, Thomas. I have never felt so desired and so happy. Thank you."

"And I love you, dear wife." He pulled her to him and kissed her, deeply and fully. "We should probably talk to the children and as much as I hate to move from this spot, start making plans to remove to Kettering. I have already sent word that we would be there in a week."

"I have never been to Kettering." She clasped her hands together. "I am looking forward to seeing our home and starting our new lives...together."

EPILOGUE

A WEEK LATER

"How much longer, my love?" Elizabeth murmured sleepily into her husband's ear. It seemed to her that they had been travelling for days.

"We arrived in Kettering about a quarter of an hour ago and should be at Rose Ridge soon." Bergen kissed her on the head and nodded at the seat across from them. "The children are still asleep. Having Clarence has slowed us rather, only because he is so young, and it was necessary to stop to water and rest him."

"He will be happy to have a home with us, I think." Elizabeth looked out of the window, watching for the wagon carrying her menagerie of animals. "I cannot believe you allowed me to keep all my pets, my beloved." She grabbed his neckcloth and tugged him down to meet her lips. "Thank you, dearest husband. I cannot believe my good fortune in finding such a loving husband." As if he had ears inside the carriage, a loud 'eeeeooooorrrree' sounded. Elizabeth held her hand to her lips and giggled softly.

"Aha! I see Clarence is in agreement!" Bergen chuckled and placed his forefinger under Elizabeth's chin, now lifting her face up to his own. "I would like one more of those, dear wife—just enough to tide me over until we are alone." His voice was low, as he drew her closer and claimed another devastating kiss.

When they at last parted, she reached up and murmured, "It meant so much to allow the children to ride in the coach with us. You will not regret it." She kissed the lobe of his ear and drew back, smiling.

"I confess, I do not feel I could regret anything about you, dear wife." Gazing out of the window, he pointed. "We are home. That is Rose Ridge."

"You told me your great-grandmother named the house, but why did she choose that name? What is the significance?"

"My understanding is that my great-grandmother found a clump of wild roses, amassed along a ridge on the property, and named the estate after it. It seems so simple, but it is true.

Elizabeth stared through the window at the property before her and knew that she was indeed home. A tall grey stone, palladium-style home stood three stories high, surrounded by lush red and white rose gardens and large grassy areas. A beautiful lake lay to the right of it, with what appeared to Elizabeth to be an elaborate Chinese garden. She wanted to pinch herself. This was going to be her new home!

A few minutes later, the carriage pulled onto the drive and the change in the terrain from dirt road to crushed oyster shells immediately woke the children, who looked about them in amazement.

"Look, there are thervanth thanding at the door." Marie leaned out of the window, trying to get a closer peek. "One, thew, three, four, five, thix, theven..." She turned to her mother. "Mama, there are tho many!"

Elizabeth glanced outside and swallowed. Indeed, a sea of people wearing white and grey were pouring from the front door to meet the carriage.

"This is a much larger home than we are used to. It will take more to keep it in order," she tried to explain, but her own level of excitement forced her closer to the window to peep over Marie's shoulders. "This is our new home, children."

The ground beneath the carriage wheels changed once more to smooth pavement and within minutes, the conveyance came to a stop and a small step was placed in front of the door before it was opened. A rather buxom man, with a bulbous nose and greying temples, greeted them with a slight bow. "Lord Bergen, Lady Bergen, welcome home."

Bergen stepped out of the door and helped Elizabeth and the children from the carriage. The senior servants were quickly introduced, and the children were soon made known to their new governess, Miss Simpson.

"How did you accomplish a place for the animals *and* a governess, all in such a short time?" Elizabeth inquired, smiling warmly at her husband.

"She is my old governess. I hope you do not mind, but since she lived nearby, Aunt Faith and I thought she could be of help, even on a temporary basis." He leaned down and kissed the top of her head. "If you are not comfortable with her appointment for any reason, you may interview to refill the position. Miss Simpson was wonderful when I was a child—strict but fair, and very engaging with her learning techniques."

Elizabeth watched the smiling older woman scoop up Ruth and take Marie's hand. Josiah hugged her and then, wearing a grin from ear to ear, followed Miss Simpson and his sisters to the nursery.

A groom stepped forward. "My lord, shall I take the animals to the stables?"

"All except for the cat." He turned to his wife, as he spoke. "Snowflake is accustomed to living in the house and shall stay with the family." Hannah moved up with the small basket containing the cat. "My lady, shall I take Snowflake to your rooms?"

"Yes. Thank you, Hannah. I will join you both shortly." As the maid left with the cat, she turned to her new husband. "I do have one small request, my lord."

"Your wish is truly my command, my love. Ask it." Bergen beamed at her.

"I would like for us to share your rooms—always. I did not enjoy such intimacy with Horace, and much has now become clearer to me since my first marriage. I want to share your bed and everything about you." She locked eyes with her husband, happy and feeling gloriously emboldened in this union.

With a wicked grin, Bergen reached down and scooped her up. Allowing herself a mock squeal, Elizabeth clung to his neck as he carried her upstairs and kicked the bedchamber door closed behind them.

"Your wish, my beautiful bride, is my command." Gently, he laid her down on the bed. "I want to savour each moment, but first…" As he spoke, he reached over to his night table and pulling a velvet box towards him, handed it to her.

"I have never accepted a gift while in bed, ready to make love, Thomas." She giggled, accepting the box. Carefully, she opened the box and gazed at the blue sapphire and diamond necklace and earrings displayed exquisitely in a platinum setting. "Oh, Thomas. This is beautiful. I will not ask how you were able to place that there," she said, laughing and pointing toward the table.

"Allow me, my lovely." He reached up and placed the necklace around her neck. "You look radiant. The diamonds and sapphires suit you." Bergen's mischievous grin sent a fluttering feeling throughout her body, igniting a warmth she rather liked. Tentatively, she touched the necklace, relishing the cool feel of it against her heated skin. She wanted more. Boldly she caught her husband's gaze, crooked her finger and wantonly invited him onto the bed. As he moved closer, she clasped her arms around his neck and pulled him down to her. "I want, Thomas, and I have waited for so long to know love like ours." She felt deliciously spoiled by her husband and the promise of their new life together. Bergen caught her hands and held them. "I shall forever endeavour to please you, dearest. You are the love I have always desired but never thought I would find."

I hope you enjoyed

EARL OF BERGEN
Make Mine An Earl Series
Book 2

**Please consider leaving a review
and/or rating on Amazon.**

Happy Reading,
Anna St. Claire

P.S. Keep Reading for a FREE PREVIEW of
EARL OF SHEFFORD
Make Mine An Earl Series
Book 3

FREE PREVIEW

EARL OF SHEFFORD

LONDON, ENGLAND ~ SEPTEMBER, 1822

"That, I believe, is the game!" Colin Nelson, the Earl of Shefford, breathed a sigh of relief. How had Bergen talked him into one more game with Lord Wilford Whitton? He already suspected the man cheated when he could, and failing that, he was a terrible loser. Tonight, the man could not cover his losses without giving up some part of his estate, having already lost both his horse and a building. A building, indeed, which now belonged to Colin, even though he was uncertain of what it looked like or its actual worth. *Nevertheless, I plan to put it to good use*, he mused. *Hell and confound it! The paper feels damp.* He glanced at the vowel before tucking it into his waistcoat pocket—making sure Whitton's perspiration had not smeared the ink before wiping his hands on his pantaloons.

"My lord, might we exchange a few words about this for a moment? Perhaps there is another way to pay you. The building has been in my family for a long while." Lord Whitton grabbed his chewed, cold cigar, which had been resting next to his empty glass, and stood up from the table. The short, red-faced lord had been huffing since he had shown his losing cards. "I have an idea and I think you might be interested in my proposal."

"I cannot imagine what else you could have. You have already wagered your horse and lost it; and now, this family building. I do not make a habit of leaving women and children homeless by winning a man's house from him." He watched Whitton wipe the sweat from his head. By now, that handkerchief had to be soaked, he thought, trying to decide how to handle the man who was growing more and more fidgety. Instinct told him it was time to leave. "I have no notion whether this building is worth the hundred pounds you owe me, but I know the area and will take a chance." Colin pushed back from the table and stood up. "The game is over. I suggest you go home." He looked around the room. Circles of cigar smoke hovered over several heads before making its way to the general haze of smoke at the ceiling. Activity ceased at the closest tables, as the players' heads turned to watch. Even the popping and crackling from the enormous fireplace across the room seemed louder and closer. He found himself buoyed by the temporary audience.

"If you will, please hear me out." Perspiration coated the man's forehead. "I should not have wagered the building."

"Yet you did," Colin responded coolly. "The gaming table has not been kind to you this night. Perhaps you should have stopped playing after you lost your horse to Lord Bergen." People like Whitton would benefit from house limits on wagers, yet they rarely put one in place.

"I thought I could win back my losses. 'Twas but a small debt," the man whined. "My horse is a thoroughbred. It should have carried me further on the wager."

Colin noted the tone of indignation steeling Whitton's voice. "Yet you lost that to a different person," Colin said with a note of astonishment even he could hear.

"He is your *friend*. How do I know the two of you have played fair?" The man sneered, the accusation clear.

From the corner of his eye, Colin observed his friend, Thomas, the Earl of Bergen, quietly signal the stalwart individual standing beside the door with a nod of his head. The last thing they needed was to dive into a mill in this hell. Colin was already regretting the decision to try out this new hell. They should have gone to the club. He did not care for public displays.

"I will give you one chance to redeem your building. If you can satisfy your entire debt by tomorrow evening—*in cash*—I will return the deed to the building. If not, consider the building payment in full."

A tall, burly man with dark hair and a trimmed beard appeared at the table. "My lord, the night has ended for you. We ask that you leave now," the bouncer said, his eyes on Whitton. For added emphasis, he pushed up each of his sleeves, revealing large, muscular arms. A tattoo of an ace of spades with a dagger across it showed on the underside of one arm.

"They have cheated me," Whitton accused, pointing a finger at Bergen and Shefford. "These are the gentlemen you should throw out —and I demand the return of the deed he stole from me," he rasped, taking a step back.

"Did you just call me a cheat?" Colin stepped forward, his voice low.

The bouncer grabbed Lord Whitton by the back of his coat. "My lord, there are windows throughout the house. If there was any cheating occurring, we would see it. I will escort you to the door. Your participation for the evening—*here, at least*—is over." With that, the guard forcibly removed the squirming, protesting man.

"You have not heard the last of me," Whitton yelled over his shoulder, before being dragged to the door.

"Well, that did not end too well," observed Colin, quietly. "I hope he finds his way home."

"Without his horse," sneered Bergen.

"Do you think he will try to take his horse? He lost it to you," Colin added wryly.

"I conjured that he might and removed the horse to the stable across the street, with ours, when I took a break from the tables earlier. I am glad I insisted on a signed bill of sale."

"Ah. Yes, that was probably wise," Colin quipped.

"Faro does not appear to be his game, Shefford," Bergen said, taking the last sip of his brandy. "Mm, I think this must be French brandy. How unusual to find it at a gaming hell." He sniffed the rim of the glass and smiled, as if confirming his point.

"I feel the need for more salubrious surroundings. What say you we head to the club?"

"That *is* funny! I am right behind you, my friend." Bergen sniggered. He picked up his coat and followed Colin.

As the two men approached the stable, a young man jumped up from where he was sitting, beneath a tree near the gate.

"M'lords," he started, brushing off his breeches. "Can I bring yer horses to ye?"

"This is the young man who has been taking care of my winnings tonight," Bergen said, chuckling.

"Me name's Danny. I'm glad to see ye, m'lord," the young man rejoined. "A shorter gentleman came fer that horse, just like ye said. I 'ad placed her in the back, in case I was with another when 'e came. He was really mad when I told him ye had taken her."

"That was good thinking. Here is a little something extra for watching our horses and being so thoughtful, Danny," Colin said, withdrawing the money from his waistcoat.

"Get away! A crown. You gents are the dog's whiskers!"

"We had a run of luck at the tables tonight and our good fortune has become your gain," Bergen added, grinning.

"Thank you," the lad said with gusto. "I'll be back in a jiffy with the horses." He pocketed the coin and hurried into the stables.

"It is interesting how Whitton's demeanor changed so rapidly," Bergen remarked thoughtfully. "You should beware. A loser's remorse can do strange things to a body. Perhaps I should apologize for talking you into one more game."

"There is no need. I won." Colin grinned. "Although I will admit I do not understand the building's worth. It could have the walls eaten through and be overrun with rats, for all I know. I plan to take a look in a day or so—if he does not find the readies for his debt."

"That was a very generous offer. You were more than fair."

"Here come our horses." Colin never felt comfortable with compliments, no matter how sincere. "I merely gave him an opportunity. The old codger seemed abnormally worried about the loss of the building."

"What are you thinking to do with a building you have yet to see, Colin?" Bergen asked, his tone one of amusement.

"Ah! Here are the horses," he said again in an attempt to deflect his friend's attention. He had an idea for the building but preferred to speak to his brother first. "It would seem our return will be slower... I suspect you will have to pull along the second horse." He eyed the mare with disfavor. "It was very well of you to move her..." Colin let his voice fade as he noticed the boy's face. Something was wrong. The hair on the back of his neck prickled. He turned around, just in time to block Lord Whitton's knife as the man thrust it towards his back. Colin's right arm received the punishing blow instead, but ignoring the pain, he pummeled Whitton with both fists, knocking him off balance. Shouting to Danny to run for help, Bergen joined him, and the two men wrestled Whitton to the ground.

"You should have that looked at," Bergen observed some minutes later as they watched a pair of constables lead Lord Whitton away in handcuffs to the lock-up. "I have never seen that man so out of control. Attacking a peer—whatever next?" He grimaced. "I cannot imagine what drove him to do such a thing."

"I will speak with the magistrate on that situation tomorrow. I have a disquieting feeling about that gentleman, and I need to make sure that they punish him for the assault," Colin muttered. "Can you help me on to my horse?"

"I will. However, I insist you come to my house. I will send for the doctor. The cut is deep and needs to be attended."

"Very well. However, I wish you will not make too much of it," Colin returned, grimacing in the other direction. *Distraction could help.* His arm felt on fire. "I would like to speak with Baxter about Whitton and make sure that he does not escape justice."

"Yes, indeed."

"Hopefully, the magistrate will send him to gaol, and they keep him there for a goodly while," Bergen added.

"He can rot there," Colin returned. "The man is dangerous and should not be among decent folk."

"He is obviously in quite deep. Unless someone owes *him*, he is not likely to have enough blunt to grease the gaoler's fist," agreed Bergen. "Whitton may be a scoundrel; however, he is also an earl. I will send word to Baxter and Morray once I have you safely home. The sooner he is under lock and key, the better."

I hope you enjoyed this FREE PREVIEW of
EARL OF SHEFFORD.

Tempted to read more?
You can find it on Amazon.

Happy Reading,
Anna St. Claire

HEART TO HEART

Dear Reader:
You are cordially invited to join my Heart to Heart Community.

Get the inside scoop on upcoming releases including the next Make Mine An Earl book.

Plus sneak peeks, freebies, contests and more.

No spammy stuff.
Only yummy stuff.

Join:
Anna St. Claire's Heart to Heart Newsletter
And get a *Noble Hearts Series Free Preview*!

Or you can visit my website:
annastclaire.com

Happy Reading,
Anna St. Claire

ABOUT THE AUTHOR

Who knew I'd become an author? Not me. But when the opportunity came, I grabbed it and approached it like I've done everything in my life—celebrating the hits and laughing at the misses. Nothing worthwhile is easy, and that includes everything in my life. But I have much to smile about—a beautiful daughter, two precious granddaughters, my adorable dogs, and my sweet husband of over thirty years. He has always supported me—including uprooting to move to the other side of Charlotte, N.C. for a life change, just when we thought we were *settled*.

If *settled* means nothing changes, then it'll never describe me. I give everything to things I enjoy—and that includes writing. In 2021, I hit the **USA Bestselling Author** list, and recently, two of my favorite books were named *RONE* **Finalists**!

My daughter avoids crowded movies with me because I'm *that woman* in the row in front of you who gleefully munches her popcorn and laughs at every hilarious scene. Loudly. Besides my family, I love chocolate, popcorn, laughter, and animals. To keep memories of my pets alive, I frequently sprinkle them in my stories as secondary characters. British and American history has always interested me, so writing historical romances in those genres always excites me.

When I was barely three, my mother moved my sister and me from New York to the Carolinas. Juggling a full-time job and full-time school, my mother became my first genuine hero—never waving the flag when things were tough. Things quickly got tough. My grandmother, who taught me to read before I started first grade, died before I was seven and I've never forgotten her.

Margaret Mitchell's *Gone with The Wind* remains one of my favorite stories, but Kathleen Woodiwiss' books, Shanna, and Ashes in The Wind, hooked me on historical romance and the dream of writing.

While I primarily write Regency romance, I enjoy almost any period in American and British history.

Connect with me via my website: www.annastclaire.com
Email: annastclaireauthor@gmail.com
Or on social media.

BOOK LIST

MAKE MINE AN EARL SERIES

EARL OF WESTON
BOOK 1

EARL OF BERGEN
BOOK 2

EARL OF SHEFFORD
BOOK 3

EARL OF HALSBURG
BOOK 4

NOBLE HEARTS SERIES

THE EARL SHE LEFT BEHIND
BOOK 1

ROMANCING A WALLFLOWER
BOOK 2

THE DUKE'S GOLDEN RINGS
BOOK 3

MY LORD, MY ROGUE

BOOK 4

<u>SILVER BELLS AND MISTLETOE</u>

BOOK 5

<u>SCANDAL BENEATH THE STARS</u>

BOOK 6

<u>NOBLE HEARTS BOX SET</u>

EMBATTLED HEARTS SERIES

<u>EMBERS OF ANGER</u>

BOOK 1

OTHER TITLES

<u>A WIDOW'S PERFECT ROGUE</u>

<u>ODDS ON AN EARL</u>

<u>THE DUKE'S GOLDEN BELLE</u>